JOE
BAKER
IS
DEAD

Joe Baker Is Dead

STORIES BY MARY TROY

University of Missouri Press

COLUMBIA AND LONDON

University of Missouri Press, Columbia, Missouri 65201
Printed and bound in the United States of America
All rights reserved
5 4 3 2 1   02 01 00 99 98

Library of Congress Cataloging-in-Publication Data

Troy, Mary, 1948–
    Joe Baker is dead : stories / by Mary Troy.
        p.   cm.
    Contents: Divine light—This too shall pass—Gloria—On
Iron Street—King Herod died of cancer—I want Myron—The
poet's daughter—Henrietta—Faithfully departed.
    ISBN 0-8262-1168-2 (pbk. : alk. paper)
    I. Title.
PS3570.R69J64   1998
813'.54—dc21   97-53057
                                                                    CIP

♾™ This paper meets the requirements of the
American National Standard for Permanence of Paper
for Printed Library Materials, Z39.48, 1984.

Cover Design (based on concept by John Troy): Mindy Shouse
Text Design: Elizabeth Young
Typesetter: BOOKCOMP
Printer and binder: Thomson-Shore, Inc.
Typefaces: Schneidler, Palatino

For credits, see page 135.

To Pierre Davis, the bee's knees,

And to Clarence and Delphine Troy,
who always gave me the world in stories.

CONTENTS

JOE
BAKER
IS
DEAD

DIVINE LIGHT

Mary Alice Conroy believed the best nuns mixed it up with the lay people, blended in while rising above. Some prayed and sang and meditated day in and day out, but when Mary Alice became a nun, she would not hide behind stone and stained glass. She would join the crowds, lightening their burdens by distributing food, interceding with the utilities, tutoring, babysitting, counseling, and all the while smiling, laughing, and praying. She would have to give up some autonomy and, of course, sex, offering it all for the glory of God, sacrificing. The poverty part would not be a sacrifice because being in the convent would allow her to eat regularly and to face each month without the cold sweat kind of worry about its bills she was growing used to.

She would join the convent because she believed in signs and considered the Fatman's heart failure a clear one, because do-gooders actually did or could do good, and because at fifty-three, she was an unemployed divorced widow whose two best friends were Sisters of Divine Light—"Divine Girls," they called themselves.

"Tell me about Mary Alice," the head of the mother house had said a few months ago when Mary Alice formally petitioned for admission. Mary Alice could have told the head Divine Girl that she had a twenty-six-year-old daughter; that for nineteen years she had been a dependable clerk and order processor for a defunct plastic-bag-making company; that she had a quarter-sized bald spot above her left temple, hidden by her naturally curly hair dyed light auburn; that she was a tone deaf, overweight

1

democrat with sagging breasts and an astigmatism who read Gerard Manly Hopkins and knew three of Shakespeare's sonnets by heart and had never seen a comet; that she had made love fourteen times, one time per man, in the seventeen years since Jack, and she considered making love, the unmarried variety without procreation as a goal, one of those things mistaken for a sin but not in fact sinful since it partook of love, which was God; or that if the convent did not take her, she would have to cash in one of her two remaining thousand-dollar IRAs by the winter solstice just to pay her rent.

Instead, she said she knew her unshakable faith in God was a gift that no amount of adversity could diminish and that she had done nothing to deserve.

The most divine of all the girls had seemed content with Mary Alice's response, but she—and they both knew it—would have accepted anyone save the criminal, the certified psychotic, or the debtor.

✳

For more than a year, Mary Alice had filled the spaces between job applications and rejection letters by hanging out with her new sister buddies and by working where she had met them, the suicide prevention hotline office. She answered the phones four nights a week with Sister Teresa Patrick and Sister William Martin who was called Bill. They were all good at it.

"I just want to die," a deep male voice said to Mary Alice on the morning she would enter the convent. In fewer than ten hours, she would knock on the front door of the mother house and humbly and officially ask to be one of them.

"Wonderful," Mary Alice said to her caller. "I envy you."

"What?" he said.

"See, I don't want to," she said. "I mean, I should want to, shouldn't I? If I believe as I profess to in the glory ever after, I should want to. But I don't. I suppose it's a fault in me. It worries me, actually."

"Who cares about you? Pay attention. I just want to die. You know, cash in my chips, kick the bucket."

"And you will. That's what's so wonderful. You want the one thing you know will happen. It's a blessing."

"I want to die *now*," he said. "Can't you understand?"

"What's your rush?" she asked. "Your body will fall apart soon enough. It's already happening. You're already dying."

It was close to 3 A.M. She would talk to this one—Ferdinand was the name he gave—until he could sleep, until five or six if she had to. If she got tired of him, she'd pass him to Teresa Patrick or Bill, let one of them have a shot. Some nights they each had callers, and they traded back and forth for variety.

This morning, Mary Alice *was* tired, not of Ferdinand and his fellow sufferers, but physically tired. Her shifts began at midnight, and she normally slept from 9 to 11:30, and then again from 6:30 to 10 A.M. That was it Thursdays through Sundays, which were in fact Friday mornings through Monday mornings. She had missed her Sunday-night rest before this Monday morning because all day Sunday she had been celebrating what her daughter, Gail, referred to as her last day of freedom.

Not that freedom was a word of much import to Mary Alice. She often called it an overrated and overdiscussed abstraction, mainly an excuse. It had been one of Jack's favorite words. But yesterday, Mary Alice followed his lead and used it as an excuse, an excuse to treat herself to a full brunch at the Ritz Carlton complete with endless Bloody Marys, followed by a matinee movie about a French detective who seduced all his witnesses, happy hour and appetizers at the airport Hilton, then a five-course feast at the most expensive four-star French restaurant in St. Louis.

After dinner, she sipped cognac in the revolving lounge overlooking the Mississippi, and prayed. Thank you for getting me into the convent in the nick of time. For the breathing room, for the way out of my financial disaster. As she prayed, she smiled at the man two tables over. Even in the low soft light, the skin sagging around his jowls seemed gray, dead. His shoulders were slumped and rounded, his neck bent under the weight of his long face. He seemed empty, a tube of toothpaste squeezed dry, a flattened and shriveled pod with no peas. She crossed to his table and sat without being asked. "Mary Alice," she said, extending her hand across his frothy drink. She did not say she would be Sister Mary Alice soon, that in fifteen and a half hours she would take the veil. She was wearing a silky black jumper over a silky white blouse because it was slimming, made her look not quite so short and squat. "Joe," he said as he pressed her hand between his warm ones, "Joe Baker." She knew she could make his life a bit happier.

Later, in the hotel room she paid for, she squeezed his testicles. They were like golf balls without the dimpled covers, hard and small. His belly was full and bouncy, but his buttocks were so small she could hold each in one hand. She would miss sex, and not just the orgasms which, she thought, were like the idea of freedom: too much was made of them. And she was not one of those women who wanted soft and warm fuzziness, wanted cuddles in order to feel loved. No, what she would miss was being connected to someone else's body, momentarily joined to a body alike and unlike hers, one functioning according to its own rhythms. Joe had an evil looking appendicitis scar, more jagged than usual, as if his doctor had coughed while cutting. His tongue and his upper arm she kissed and licked tasted of sage. The nail of the big toe on his right foot was sharp and cut her ankle.

Mary Alice went straight from Joe to the suicide prevention offices above the Ford dealership on Manchester Road. Not to repeat myself, she told God, but I'll miss that. Still, I'll offer it up, my desires will become my sacrifice. More like Able than Cain. She used to laugh at her girlfriends during Advent or Lent when they gave up carrots or rutabagas instead of Coca Colas and chocolate bars. Sacrifices had to be real to matter.

She also argued with Jack about it. He believed in the other person sacrificing, taking a chance, risking his comforts for a principle. "I do it," he would say. "I put myself on the line over and over."

"Because that's you," she said. "It would be a sacrifice for you to keep quiet every now and then, to go along to keep the peace. Like at Calverton." Calverton was the military high school where Jack had taught English for almost an entire semester. On the second day of classes, he organized a protest against the military part of the school, eventually convincing some of the boys not to drill. Many of Jack and Mary Alice's young friends laughed at him for that. "Hell, Jack," they said, "didn't you know it was a military school? I mean, was this affront a big surprise?"

Jack, the activist, pacifist humanitarian, the free love practitioner, rescuer of the runaways, spreader of diseases—he'd given her crabs at least twice—and eventual millionaire and television commercial idiot, had come from a long line of what he called ignorant, stubborn brawlers. His two brothers were often under court orders to stay away from specific women, and his father's body was a tapestry of scars, mementoes of barroom skirmishes. Jack rejected their physical ways, but carried the fighting genes. Life was for fighting, but for Jack, the fight was with the establishment instead of the drunk across the bar.

Still, she often thanked God for her fourteen years as Jack's wife. Jack used to talk faster than his mind or mouth could work, spit when he grew excited, and she had had him longer than any of his subsequent wives. He had given her Gail.

Children were blessings, frosting on the cake. She and Jack and all their friends had agreed on that way back when children started coming. Amid discussions, in rooms filled with thick, sweet smoke, about whether you could see yourself in a mirror if you traveled faster than the speed of light, they'd talked child raising. You should protect, feed, clothe your child. Perhaps educate—there was some disagreement about that—but not mold. Well, Mary Alice had tried not to mold, but she had given Gail advice: act as you believe all others should for the world to be such that you want to live in it.

God gave advice, too, and that after having created man in God's own image. Still, He, She, or It did not feed, clothe, or protect. In fact, God seemed to enjoy throwing obstacles up and watching the poor dumb creatures maneuver around them while being good. Sorry, Mary Alice said to God as she turned into the suicide prevention hotline office parking lot. Don't think I'm complaining. You have been a big help to me lately.

Teresa Patrick opened a bottle of Cold Duck as soon as Mary Alice entered the small office.

"Lots of orders go to Guatemala, Sri Lanka, or Angola for the new recruits, someplace where women need free education," Bill said as a toast. "But not us." She sneered, bringing a side of her top lip all the way up to a nostril. Mary Alice had also seen her turn her eyelids inside out and wiggle her ears. "No, not us," Bill continued. "We take middle-aged, unemployed clerks."

"Here, here," Teresa Patrick said, and they all drank. "Just what we need, another oldie. Soon our biggest expense will be diapers."

"You know who changes the diapers, don't you?" Bill asked.

"The postulants," Mary Alice said, happy to know the answer. She had heard it before.

"Postulants?" Teresa Patrick cried, throwing her blonde braid back over her shoulder. "Do you have a frog in your pocket? Wise up, Mary Alice. You're it. The entire new class."

"So were you," Bill said to Teresa Patrick. "Only you were a skinny, scared girl. Not like Big Mama here." She swept an arm out, and said, "Ta-da! Big Mama, the new, but not young, blood." But the gesture was too extravagant for the tiny office, for the safety of the decorations on the bookcase behind her. She knocked Saint Peter onto the floor and his head broke cleanly off.

"Just some old man statue," Bill said as she bent to pick up the two pieces.

"Another one bites the dust," Teresa Patrick said.

Bill replaced Saint Peter, now headless, on the bookcase. "Who's responsible for this religious paraphernalia anyway?"

It was not a real question; Mary Alice had confessed to it before. "Me," she said.

She had found Peter and the others—Saints Jude, Joseph, Francis of Assisi, Anthony, the Angel Gabriel—at a yard sale the day before Jack's death. Another sign. She had lined them all up on her kitchen table and begged for help. "I can't find work. I have no direction, no money. I won't be able to afford my rent soon. I'll have to work at McDonalds *and* Burger King if I want to keep my car and my apartment. You're all experts at something, all you guys, so help me. Get cracking. Tell me what to do."

The next day, Jack's heart muscles shuddered, knotted up, and went slack, and so she was a widow, able to join her buddies and devote her life to helping others. She never knew which of the six convinced God to take Jack just when it could help her the most, so she enshrined them all in the suicide prevention hotline office.

Jack had not been really fat, at least not when Mary Alice protested and worked with him to expedite CO status for those who would not go to Southeast Asia and kill. They had worked with priests, ministers, and underground networks that hid young men whose time had run out. Jack was merely chubby then, his back and shoulders like twice risen bread dough. His hands were wide and he kicked his legs out as he walked, a mannerism he had developed as a child to keep his thighs from rubbing together and the fabric of his trousers from whistling or humming with each rub. His black eyes were intense, lively, and even the curls hanging on his forehead bounced with energy. She loved him for his beliefs, for his desire to help others, and because he needed her. She kept track of his meetings, typed his letters, showed him how to fill out the forms. She made copies of all the paperwork and filed them alphabetically. He orated, dreamed, and inspired.

She believed in free love, and so gave herself to him freely right after the ecumenical prayer service for the recent war dead where she met him. That was all free love meant to her. The whole time he was around, she never wanted anyone else. He called her voluptuous, the epitome of womanhood.

"Making love is such intense pleasure," he said after the second time. They were lying on a thin, heavily stained, twin sized mattress they had thrown down on the floor moments before. They were in the basement of Holy Cross church where Jack had sympathizers upstairs in the rectory. "We shouldn't horde it, give it to just one person," he said. "We love many people, and we should spread it around, right?"

"Right," she said. She was keeping her eyes on a spider crawling erratically around on the beams above. She was afraid it would fall off just when it was over her. Even before their wedding, held upstairs in Holy Cross proper a year later, Mary Alice knew Jack made love with many others, was spreading love to those in need. Those in need were usually thin blondes, innocent and confused-looking like Teresa Patrick or the girl who played the guitar at Mary Alice and Jack's wedding and led the congregation in "Kumbaya."

∗

It was Gail's ninth birthday, after the family party, when he told her one of the runaways he had been counseling was pregnant. He and Mary Alice were at the sink, doing the party dishes. She washed and he dried. "I'm probably the father," he said.

"Probably?" She held her hands down in the cooling sudsy water, hoping for an out.

"Well, OK," he said, "I know it. I am."

She understood then that the advice of forsaking all others had been given as a practical way of avoiding complication. God was a realist. She kept her eyes on the dishwater. "Give her a break," she said. "Marry her." She hoped it didn't sound bitter. She had not meant it to be.

∗

Ferdinand was Mary Alice's only caller of the night, and she had finished her first glass of Cold Duck and was starting on her second when he rang in. She finished her second glass by the time he hung up after promising to stay alive until at least one more full moon and to call back. By the end of the conversation, she had been listening to her own words echo in her head. She could have been talking in her sleep. The Cold Duck was making her lips numb.

"Want a refill?" Teresa Patrick asked, the bottle tipped over Mary Alice's glass.

"Don't mind if I do," Mary Alice said.

"I'm offering, even though you've cluttered this place up with plaster of Paris men."

"I'm accepting, even though I don't drink much as a rule."

"I know," Bill said. "We've some who do. As if it's a rule. 'Thou shalt drink thyself into oblivion as often as possible.' "

"Postulants usually get the puke detail," Teresa Patrick said.

"Postulants?" Mary Alice asked.

∗

Her eye muscles would not work on the drive to her apartment. The objects in the foreground were outlined in black as if they had been cut from a dark background and pasted on. The gas station she passed shimmied, vibrated. Once she thought her eyes had closed, so she struggled to open them again, forcing the lids up with a finger, only to discover they had been open all along. A young woman in a van was tailgating her, so she turned right, then left onto a narrow residential road, more peaceful than the main thoroughfare. These were the homes of the well-to-do, some with five-car garages and tri-level decks out back.

"Holy God, we praise thy name," she sang to keep awake. "Lord of all, we bow before thee. Infinite thy vast domain." She had known the Cold Duck would be too much. She had acted like Jack, no restraint. She would not like to live in a world where everyone was like her, driving drunk and tired. Or like Jack who had never thought how his actions would affect anyone, even himself, before he and a troubled young girl would commune with nature on a blanket on a bluff above the Mississippi River. "There are many expressions of love," he would tell the young girl. Mary Alice knew, because he had told her the same. "But this is the most profound, the closest to divine."

Though Mary Alice was not a drinker, had not even over-indulged to drown her sorrow when Jack left, she did drink, had wanted to become drunk, the evening she saw the first Fatman commercial. There was Jack, on television, vaulting over the back of a couch and crashing down on it. Sprawling, wallowing about on recliners and side chairs were also in his repertoire, as was jumping on a bed and leaning on a dinette set. "Even I can't hurt this!" he shouted. "The Fatman can't hurt this." It was painted on his trucks: "The Fatman can't hurt this!"

"How did this happen?" Mary Alice asked him after enough beers to make the call.

"It's a fluke, Babe," he'd said. "Serendipity, as is everything. Fate. Karma. What was meant to be. I'm as surprised as you."

The truth was his new and third father-in-law had owned a small cut-rate furniture store in the city, and he sold it to Jack cheap. An old pal of Jack's, one he and Mary Alice had saved from

Vietnam long ago, had grown up to be a marketing specialist, and he told Jack fat was where it was at. Fat would make the difference. In four years, Jack opened four new stores. He also took a fourth wife.

And fat had made the difference for Mary Alice, too. Enough of it clogging the arteries, weighing down Jack's heart, had allowed Mary Alice to become a Sister of Divine Light. God helped when He or She or It had a mind to.

Jack's four children and their four mothers had been brought together for the reading of the will. Jack had insisted. "A party," he had written in his will, "is up there on the holiness scale. Christ loved 'em. Look at that marriage feast business." That marriage feast business, as he called it, was why Mary Alice had had to wait for him to die before she could enter the convent. He would not agree to an annulment. A divorce was one thing: a merely legal term, a bow to the establishment. An annulment was entirely different: an admission that the sacrament of marriage had not really been blessed by God, a denial of the marriage feast.

"And though he knew he would die the next day," the will read, "Christ had a dinner party for his pals, even rented a room for it. So this should be a party. Get to know one another. Have fun." Other than the lawyer, Jack's two unmarried brothers, the four mothers who already knew or knew of one another, and the four children, there was one other guest. The shy little Asian girl who had done his books showed up.

"I'm carrying his child," she said. "He told me there are many kinds of love. He said this was the closest to divine." They all believed her.

In his will, Jack left his love to all his wives and children, even to his brothers and—"what the hell," he'd written—to his lawyer, but said his business was to be sold and the profits added to his estate and the entire amount divided among a few specifically named shelters for the indigent. He said he knew none of those present really cared for money or for some stupid furniture business.

"Rotten son-of-a-bitch," one brother said. "I'd like to kill him."

*

Mary Alice opened her eyes seconds before she hit the house, but the impact was what woke her, caused her head to bob on her neck. She was confused, but knew she had hit something. Not a house. Surely not. The house was standing. Her head stopped bobbing. There was no blood. She closed her eyes, and when she opened them again, the corner of the house, gray siding joined and overlapping, was in her unbroken front windshield as before. Some of the siding was torn. The hood of her car, though, was as wide and nearly as smooth as always. She looked behind her and saw tire ruts in the damp brown grass all the way from the road, twenty feet away. She rested on what seemed a gravel turnaround. A cry? Had she heard one? A yelp? A scream? It must have been hers. There was no one else around.

She should get out; she should knock on the door. It was only 7 A.M., and they may not be up yet. "Hello," she'd say. "I hit your house." Now she was being silly. What did the words matter, how it was said? But surely, her hitting had jolted those inside enough to have awakened them. If anyone was inside. If no one was home, there was only one thing to do. Go back, walk back so the evidence remained intact, and call the police. That was the only possibility. But surely not everyone out here worked so early. Surely a neighbor had already called the police, and they were on their way now. They would ticket her, fine her, arrest her for drunk driving, reckless driving, negligence, probably a few other infractions she was not aware of. They would book her. She would have to borrow from Gail to pay her fine, her bail. Her insurance would pay for the house except for the deductible, then cancel her. The Divine Girls would not want her as one of them before it was all taken care of, and maybe not at all because DWI was a big crime, and though DWS, driving while sleepy, was not, it should be, and she had been doing both, DWI and DWS.

She opened her car door to begin her walk back to the road and the police station, wherever it was. She put one foot down on the gravel and saw the tail, a black one with a white tip. There was a short-haired dog under her. She closed the door. She had killed a dog. If it was not dead, she would hear it crying. She did not want to see it. She had killed someone's dog, a loved and treasured pet. It must have been chained or tied up, otherwise it would have moved out of the way. She had not been going fast. The house was barely touched. Her car was still running, so she knew it was not hurt much, but the siding was torn and the dog was dead.

And there were hidden problems. She knew most problems were hidden. The pipes, the wires, the ceilings, and the roof may have been knocked out of joint, out of place, maybe just enough to cause expensive problems. Structural problems. And the dog was dead. The owners may want more than her insurance covered, and they may sue her for criminal negligence, and the Divine Girls would pray for her, help her if they could as they helped the luckless, but would probably not let her join. She had only six hundred dollars left in her account and had planned to take that to the sisters, who were running out of money. It was like a dowry. She was to be a bride of Christ, but now the wedding was off.

And what kind of people would leave a dog out on a chain and not even be home in case it got tangled up on something? People who didn't love the dog, not really. People who would pretend it was a champion or pedigree at the trial. And they must be rich because only rich people lived out here. They were probably lawyers—a pair of them with an expensive dog of some kind they did not love, one they chained up just so it would get hit and they'd have someone to sue.

But Mary Alice knew she was wrong.

Fifteen minutes. She had been sitting in her car for fifteen minutes. Clearly no neighbors had called the police. Amazing that her mistake had gone undetected. Miraculous.

She backed up, trying not to think of what she was doing to the dog's body. If it were a person under her car, she would stay, turn herself in. Surely God knew that. She turned around before the gravel ended, and drove back up over the grass and mud. Yes, she would not run if it were a person. No matter the consequences. God must believe that because Mary Alice knew it was true. If you're going to hold this against me, she said to God, You'll have to take into account all the good I've done, all the lives I've saved.

She was only a small glob of smart cells in a cluttered world, a clump of atoms on the edge of a spinning mass of gas. Not worthy of God's attention. God was large, all encompassing. In fact, she said to God, You don't expect much from us anyway. You made us confused, selfish, most of all, frightened. Frightened of You, yes, but also and mainly of our own tenuous survival.

Forgive me, she said as she pulled back onto Antelope Drive. I do know what I'm doing.

THIS TOO SHALL PASS

Bucknell Pastor sat up, blinked twice, and his ex-wife Cindy disappeared. She had been sitting cross-legged at the end of his bed, wearing her pink baby dolls, thermometer in her mouth, her head tilted to one side so her butterscotch-colored hair just caressed a shoulder. Though he had not seen her in the flesh in baby dolls for close to two years, he woke up to her in them, the lace around the neck line ragged, at least once a week.

He told Joan Hampton he had nightmares. "I dream about my ex," he said and laughed. "Real nightmares." The nightmare part was that she disappeared.

Joan picked him up and drove him to work most weekdays because she lived only a few miles farther south, and because their employer promoted carpooling by assigning Joan and others like her parking spaces close to the side entrance. Their employer was In Touch, Incorporated, a direct mail advertising firm that Bucknell called despicable and horrid to himself and *not a bad place*, or *as good as any*, or *the old salt mines* when talking to others. The job had been Cindy's idea. He was a married man after all, she had said when the opportunity came up two months after their wedding, because one of his mother's men friends was an original In Touch investor. Cindy was impressed with the insurance benefits, especially the maternity ones, and the profit-sharing plan that would help send their children to college. That was six years ago when she wrote speeches and press releases for a senator they had met where they'd met each other, the headquarters for the Coalition for a Clean World. Cindy knew her job depended upon the senator's re-elections. She knew Bucknell needed something permanent.

"I take an aspirin before bed," Joan said. "I don't dream at all. Try it, Buck." They sat at an intersection two blocks from In Touch, waiting for a left arrow.

"Bucknell," he said to her as he often had. "Buck's the name of a guy whose jeans are too low slung, who spits from his car window."

"Wave when we go past Joe's," she said. "I'll honk and you wave."

Joe was Joe Baker, the owner of a produce store across from In Touch and Joan's lover. Joan was in her fifties, twenty-three years older than Bucknell. She was a frumpy, dumpy woman with frizzed but style-less hair, a body that seemed built by mounding clay on two toothpicks, and a preference for sweaters with life-sized geraniums, pot included, appliquéd across the front, or for sweatshirts that played tunes when squeezed in the right places. Yet she had a lover. A married lover, the best kind, she claimed. Joe was her third, and he represented, as the other two had, totally selfless love, pure love. "I expect and get nothing in return," Joan had explained. "None of them give me other than momentary pleasure twice a week if I'm lucky. I give without hope of a return. Pure love."

"My ex had an affair with a married man. She married him," Bucknell had answered.

"She was selfish, greedy. A no-class kind of person. Forgive me for saying so, Buck."

"Bucknell," he had said.

Now he waved in the direction of Joe's produce store, which was darker and dingier than usual.

At In Touch, for In Touch, he wrote the in-house organ designed to keep the copywriters, computer programmers, data analysts, account execs, and mail sorters happy and motivated to work harder. He wrote about softball teams and productivity awards and the joy of carpooling. He related family anecdotes and chronicled the births, deaths, marriages, and weight losses of the employees and their relations. He was working this week on a theme issue—survival. He was known as a pleasant guy with clever ideas and a good attitude. He was good looking in an average way—medium height and weight, medium brown hair worn in the traditional part-on-the-left-side style, medium brown eyes, a brownish moustache, and no unusual features. A regular guy is how his coworkers would have described him. Someone you hardly notice, some of them would have said, while others would have called him ideal, part of the flow, bobbing along deep in the mainstream.

They did not know he saw his ex-wife sitting on his bed, did not know he saw the walls of his office move in closer and closer, though he could not prove it by the measuring tape he brought in. And he had seen his desk turn into a malamute and snap at his hand, growl when he approached. Often he saw an old woman in pale clothes, her white hair streaming behind her as she stood on the side of the highway, hitchhiking. She vanished each time he stopped for her. They did not know he had sluggish sperm.

He began writing from his interview with an account exec whose country home had been ravished two years ago when the Mississippi, Missouri, and Meramec Rivers all overran their banks. The home was just now livable again, thanks to his wife's decorating skill and to a flood insurance policy which, thank God, the account exec had had. Bucknell had already finished his story on the woman in payroll who had survived a mastectomy—thank God—and the copywriter whose riding mower had fallen on him. He got around just fine now with his artificial knee; thank God for the doctors and his insurance policy.

Yes, they all seemed to think God was in charge, and Bucknell's mother was the same. "God was with me," she would say when she entered his apartment before the dinner he prepared for just the two of them each Sunday. "I got all the green lights." "God must hate the ones who got the reds," he would say to upset her, and she would shake her head, press her lips together tighter than usual.

Perhaps he should ask the Big Boss in the Sky to find him a job he could be proud of. The junk In Touch mailed out, the mail people threw out almost as soon as it darkened their boxes, the trees sacrificed to advertise *Gone with the Wind* dolls and key rings with police whistles in them: all that was discouraging. An old college pal worked for the big weapons manufacturer that kept the St. Louis economy alive. He did something with integrated systems and smart bombs, and Bucknell thought his contribution to chaos and destruction so obvious that quitting should have been an easy choice. He used to say so to Cindy.

"But war is not all bad," Cindy had said to him more than once. "Look at Hitler. How could we have kicked his ass without all those wonderful weapons, big bombs?"

"How could he have threatened without his wonderful weapons?" Bucknell answered, but he was not an activist. Good Lord, he'd been writing vapid columns for six years. When he did not dream of Cindy, he dreamed of himself wading through slick full-color catalog covers, mounds of them, sinking and drowning in special offers, being chased by articles on baby showers for the receptionist.

Bucknell read his notes for the survival article. The account exec had seen the flood as character building. "It's what's in here," he had said, pointing to his breastbone. "You survive disaster because of what's in here, what's inside." Cindy had been concerned with the inside, too, with Bucknell's insides. "Let what's in there come out," she said often, sometimes through tears. She meant about the potential baby. She wanted feeling as well as performance. "If there is anything in there," she would add. He had gone along with the tests, had found out that his sperm the specialists called sluggish were not impossibly sluggish, could fertilize under the very best of conditions, like planting beans at the dark of the moon, he thought. So he had tried to impregnate her when her temperature was right, had worn loose underpants, had cut down on, cut out actually, sex for fun, saving those sacred sperm for the big job. He had done all that, but had not seemed interested, Cindy complained. She accused him of not really wanting a child.

It was like asking for a puppy for Christmas, he explained. You were just as likely to get a stuffed animal, or worse, a kitten. You couldn't have your heart set on the puppy. Besides, he would want to add, my sperm are sluggish, our chances are slim. He knew better, though, than to remind her of his shortcoming. She cried often in those days, whimpering that she needed someone who shared her enthusiasm, and he thought her insides came out too often, too easily. There seemed to be no boundary between inside and outside with Cindy.

Joan interrupted his work. She looked frumpier than usual as she stood in the door of his ever-shrinking office. Her face was puffy and red, her eyes gleamed. He saw her pick him up by the scruff of the neck, twirl him around twice, then slam him down on his keyboard. He must not have waved hard enough at Joe's this morning. He was heavier than she, though not by much he guessed, but it would be what Cindy called an adrenaline thing, like when mothers lifted city buses off their trapped children. But instead, Joan cried. What had seemed rage was sorrow. She wept so she leaked at all the seams, leaving puddles on top of her cheeks, tributaries running down her neck.

"Know why Joe did not wave back this morning?" She hiccupped as she talked. "He's dead."

"Joe?" he said. "Dead?" Did every man's death diminish him? Was Joe a clod of importance? No. Even his produce was bad, his carrots limp and his bananas mushy. But he was Joan's passion, her selfless and pure love, and though Joan was not exactly a friend, she was crying in his door. He hugged her, told her to sit, used his coffee cup to give her water from the fountain in the hallway. "How?" he asked.

"An explosion. Last night. In his head. A vessel popped like a balloon."

"Who told you?"

"Someone at his home. I called because the store was closed. Didn't you notice it seemed deserted as we drove by? On the phone I asked if something was wrong, pretending to be a customer, and the woman, a daughter-in-law perhaps, said lots was wrong." Joan paused, rubbed her eyes, leaned her head back along the edge of his roll-about desk chair. "Thank the Blessed Virgin Mary he wasn't with me last night. He had said he would come if he could get away." She stood and wiped her nose on the back of her hand.

After a few more sobs and dear Gods, she left his office, went to her own in the research department where today she would cry instead of searching for connections among catalog subscribers.

There it was again. Thank God. Thank the Blessed Virgin Mary. Dear God. Was it God's will that Bucknell, at not even thirty, not quite thirty, was entrenched in a life he would have chosen last if given the choice of all possible lives? Sure, from the outside it seemed okay, perhaps even desirable. His social life was full: he spent time with women, with his pals, talking about football and potholes and crime and the latest movies, laughing when appropriate at their jokes about idiots fucking or fucking idiots. He did not tell any of them he saw his walls moving or that he had seen his grade school principal, Sister Corine, hiding behind his shower curtain a week ago as he sat on his toilet reading an article on the passenger trains of a bygone era.

✳

"Go to the funeral with me," Joan said on the way home.

"I hardly knew him."

"I don't want to go alone. I'm afraid of seeming conspicuous. A mysterious woman mourner and all that. No sense letting the cat out of the bag now. We can say we were customers who will miss his service."

"What's the point of a funeral anyway?" Morbid affairs, Bucknell thought. Death worship.

"That from a Catholic?"

"My training's a blur."

"To pray him to heaven. To make us left behind feel better. You can pray for me. It's Saturday morning at nine. I'll pick you up at eight-thirty."

"I have a date Friday. I may not be home by Saturday morning," he said. Her name was Mara. She lived in his building, and they had met at the coin-operated washers. She was fixing dinner and his job was to pick out the movie. A night on her couch was what she had planned, a romantic movie no doubt what she wanted.

Since his divorce, he had not yet made the first move, had not had to. Women liked him. Even Cindy liked him, claimed she did still. Though Mara was young and her soft hair shone in the fluorescent lights of the laundry room, she was not Cindy. Cindy was beef in a red curry sauce, or in her sweeter moods, a butterscotch sundae with the works. Mara was toasted cheese. He pictured cuddling with a toasted cheese; there would be grease spots on the couch. The image was his mother's fault. She had given him a subscription to *Gourmet Magazine* to celebrate the finality of his divorce. "The days of bachelors just eating frozen dinners are long gone, dead," she had said. "Dead and buried," his mother always said of the bad old days when men did nothing.

"Look," he said as Joan dropped him off, "I'll go if I can." It was only Thursday. Sister Corine may ambush him, whack his hands, make him stay in from recess before then.

Two pieces of mail were in his box. No junk. The first was a letter from a medical textbook publisher in town. Thanks but no thanks for his application to be an editor/proofreader. They had picked someone with more textbook experience. "Well, fine," he said out loud to the Human Resources Director. Textbooks were almost as wasteful as slick catalogs. Didn't the publishers change editions every few years? Didn't they dump the old texts in landfills and let the acetate overlays of skeletal and muscular systems try to rot, slower than what they depicted would have?

The other piece of mail was from Cindy. Cindy Watanabe, the return address sticker read, no longer Pastor. He had last seen her at Joe Baker's, where they were both buying brussels sprouts, a taste they shared. She had said then she wanted to be friends, she still liked him. Her stomach was larger and riper than the melons behind her. "I forgot you shopped here," he said, knowing she would not believe it. "What's wrong?" she joked. "Did you want sole custody of our produce man?" He doubted they could be friends, but he would be agreeable. He had always been agreeable. After all, he had shaken Mits's hand— Mits's mitt—had said I hope you make her happy, something like that, when he had known he should have said *pregnant*,

I hope you make her pregnant. But in fact he had not hoped for either.

Mits Watanabe was a gardener, a landscape architect he said, who had taught the Yoga relaxation class at the Y Cindy had taken at her doctor's suggestion. The doctor was right; the class had helped Cindy conceive. Mits relaxed her, and what was more, his sperm were not sluggish. He had two children at home to prove his ability.

Bucknell opened the card from Cindy Watanabe and saw a picture of her newborn son complete with a pointed head, a thatch of black hair, no chin, and single-lidded eyes. Congratulations, Mrs. Watanabe, he would write, on the birth of your ugly child. Was that being friendly? Maybe he should leave out the congrats, be honest as friends were supposed to be. What an ugly child you have. Or, dear Cindy, did you know it would be so ugly?

And as Bucknell looked at the photo of Raymond Chieko Watanabe, he saw the baby wink, then close both eyes. When he looked up, the Blessed Virgin Mary was sitting on his couch. Her legs were crossed, and her hands were resting loosely on her lap. She looked serene, looked like a woman waiting to be offered a cup of tea.

"We hear you," she said.

"Hear what?" He knew who she was. The halo gave her away.

"We hear your prayers, Buck. Don't think we don't."

"Bucknell," he said. "You look like Cindy would in blue and white robes."

"I'm known for my beauty."

"I don't pray. I don't even believe."

"The hell you don't. And what else do you call your agonizing dreams and so-called thoughts, your yearnings, if not prayer?"

"You can curse?"

"I can do anything. No restrictions. The Immaculate Conception, remember?"

"Vaguely."

"I'm busy. I'll get right to the point. I could tell you exactly where you've failed so far, what and why you have screwed up, but I'll have to let that wait, be a big surprise to you on judgement day. So, here's the plan. Get out of that job. You're right about it. It's an abomination. A sham. Resign tomorrow. I have something better in store for you."

"Like?"

"Like there's a big charity in town run by some well-meaning but incompetent laypersons. It needs to raise money. It needs a writer. As rampant capitalism is not your thing, it needs you."

Like Sister Corine and the hitchhiker and the snarling dog-desk, she disappeared as suddenly as she had appeared. But the yellow pages were on his coffee table, opened to page 1102, Shelters and Food Pantries. Beside *Loaves and Fishes* was an arrow leading to a sideways-written margin note: "they need a writer, call." The BVM had neat penmanship, pretty like a nun's.

So he called, and was told to come in on Saturday afternoon. His call was miraculous, the guy on the phone said. How did he know they needed someone? They had only decided a few hours earlier. The problem was they could not pay much, but Bucknell could make do on it. It was God's will he was single, no children, he thought as he hung up. A plan, a design was apparent, or could be if looked at or for. And he wondered, should he believe— did he?

Mara and he were bored by each other. That much was obvious. Static cling and fabric softener may have been all they shared. She may have wanted urbane wit and so found his company self as typical and mundane as it was. She may have wanted passion, perhaps intimacy. Clearly, she was disappointed, yawning often, looking over his shoulder at her sunburst wall clock. He could have given her the real Bucknell, but was the real one what he was or what he had been? Cindy had told him he was not who he was in the present, but who he had been, the sum of his past. He had been married to Cindy in the past, but had not been happy then either because of the thermometer and her tears and his job. He could go further back to the days of his illness, the rheumatic fever that possessed him at twelve and the resulting frailty his mother was sure would linger forever. She sprinkled him with Lourdes water each morning of his high school years. He awoke to drops of cold water hitting his nose until he went away to college. Anyway, Mara was bored by Bucknell, past and present, probably future if he had one, and he was in bed by ten-thirty, alone. He expected the BVM to return, to ask how the call went, to give him some interview pointers, but she didn't show.

Bucknell paid little attention during the funeral mass but instead stared at the statue of Mary, her foot on a snake. He thought she was breathing. His interview at Loaves and Fishes was scheduled for noon. Perhaps they'd give him lunch, the free one all the bums got, warm, rib-sticking slop. He noticed the rest of the congregation whispering, tsk-tsking, while the priest ended the mass not by anointing the casket and turning it around to go out head first, but by talking about Joe Baker's personality. It was just not done, not now. Bucknell could see the widow fidgeting, her silver head shaking under its black veil. When it was finally over, the mass and the ending indignity, he turned to follow the others out behind the casket. Just as he turned, the statue of Mary turned too, faced him and gave him thumbs up. He couldn't lose.

✳

"Are you a practicing Catholic?" the young, pimply faced man behind the desk asked.

"Yes," Bucknell lied, assuming the Virgin would approve of one so small. After all, this kid who had been studying for the priesthood before changing his mind and opting for social work, this *acting* director, had probably not conversed with the Virgin in person as Bucknell had. The kid had not been chosen.

"We need someone who can reach people. We need ads that convince people to help."

"Play on guilt and all that," Bucknell said. "Sure. I know."

"We like to think of it as appealing to man's better nature."

"Sounds good. I'm sure I can do it."

"Great." The kid stood, seemed to paw the air. He wanted to shake hands. "I have to have board approval, but that's just a formality. Welcome aboard, Buck. Can I call you Buck?"

"No."

As simple as that. It was true what they said. It paid to have connections. He had known it, of course, had been hired at In Touch through his mother's friend's help, but the BVM, now that was a connection. As connected as one could get. That is, if he believed those myths, and he may as well. Of course, he would make twelve thousand a year less, and some people—Cindy for one, and his mother, Joan, and probably even Mara for two, three, and four—would not consider it a wise decision, a good direction. But it was moving, and up or down, back or forth, even sideways, moving was moving. Cindy had moved, changed her name and life in less than two years.

While driving home from Loaves and Fishes, he saw his hitch-hiker again, this time in double exposure. She was twins. They were both barefoot and, though it was a sunny day, the February wind carried a slight chill. He knew he had to stop, mirage or no mirage. Naturally, they vanished as he pulled over.

✳

"This is my last day," he told Joan on Monday. "I'm going to quit after lunch. Effective immediately."

"I'll lose my parking space."

"Them's the breaks."

"It's idiotic of you to quit, especially to work in some soup kitchen."

"Actually, they serve fried chicken." He had been surprised when the kid said so, disappointed not to have been asked to dine.

"That's nice," she said. "Give the homeless a cholesterol problem."

✳

"My mother is sick. She needs constant care. I have to quit to attend to her." He talked to the Director of Employee Motivation. I have to use my talents for good, he told himself. That, or put a bushel over them.

"If you keep your job, you can afford better care for her. Think about it. Not that I don't understand filial love. I'd run into a burning building to save my own mother."

Bucknell hovered near the light fixture, looked down on the scene. Why had he lied? He meant to tell the truth. "I have to quit," he said.

"Your face is flushed. Are you okay, Buck?"

"Bucknell," he said. "For six years I've been Buck*nell*. I'm fine. I'm leaving. I have to."

The Director of Employee Motivation shrugged his shoulders. "It would be better if you gave a few weeks' notice, trained your replacement."

"Sorry," Bucknell said. At Loaves and Fishes his desk would not snarl at him.

✳

"I'm ready," Bucknell said to the kid whose pimples seemed more virulent than ever. It was Tuesday morning, early. He wanted to put in a whole day, start right in pulling the bleeding hearts' strings. Under one arm he carried a shoe box containing his personal desk decorations—an acrylic pen holder, a coffee cup with nothing written on it, a five-year-old picture of Cindy, and a four-inch-high white plastic statue of the BVM he had found in his mother's kitchen.

"Ready?" the kid asked, and then blushed. "Oh, you see, after the board meeting yesterday, the director had an idea. His son's at St. Louis U., a junior majoring in professional writing."

Bucknell sat, set his shoe box at his feet.

"His name's Peter," the kid continued. "He'll write for us free. For college credit. We called St. Louis U., and it's all arranged. Saves us money, you know. That's what counts."

Bucknell placed his head in his hands.

"Someone was supposed to have called you. Don't cry, Buck."

But Bucknell was not crying. He was squeezing his eyes shut, calling Mary. Come back. Right now. Busy or not. Help me, he said. Tell me what to do now. Well, even he who had forgotten most of what Sister Corine and others had drilled into him by rote and whacks knew that God worked in mysterious ways, knew that all prayers were answered, knew that one had only to ask. He need not worry. If he saw the barefoot twins, he would stop again. If he saw Cindy, he would say her child was handsome. If he prayed for himself, he would throw in an extra for Joe Baker's soul. He was like a lily of the fields. He would get by. It was only a matter of time before Mary appeared and gave him another bright idea.

GLORIA

In the beginning, there was a funeral, Gloria would say to herself later, early the morning following and referring to the day that turned out worse than bad. She paced her living room and dining room and wondered. Was it her mother's craziness or too much togetherness? Was it the flag pole or the Gulf War he was nearly alone in protesting? Surely it could not have been what he said about jokes because it never hurt to laugh. Perhaps it should have been expected. "I keep seeing your mother's face," he had said a few weeks ago. "In my dreams. The terrible Galveston face."

She nodded then, had said, "I know," until he sighed deeply.

"No. You do not know."

Gloria knew that if the end of the world came at the end of the day, long past sunset and the expandable cocktail hour—no matter how many hours it expanded to—if the end of the world came then, there would be signs. The planets would spin crazily, birds would fall from their boughs, and of course, woe to her with child. Or was it that what had always been lovely sex could not produce a child, lovely or not? So, too, today, there should have been signs: a penny discovered on the sidewalk, head down perhaps but picked up anyway. Bad luck, her father would have said. Maybe Babs being almost out of gas and deliberately not filling up, wanting to see how low the needle would go and so making Gloria nervous was a sign. And they had sat in front of Anna Rower, who all during mass had coughed up mucous balls that must have been the size of small rodents.

They had gone to Joe Baker's funeral that morning at Holy Cross because they were parishioners and they took their duty to bury the dead seriously. Neither Gloria nor Babs had known Joe well, but they had served on a few committees with the widow, Sheila Baker. She had once made Gloria and Babs, the former sisters Duff, roll their eyes and bite the insides of their cheeks because she spoke as if sex were as unpleasant a duty as making payments on a new dinette set. But sex, the sisters knew, was one of the three reasons for marriage, one of the three they had decided upon years earlier before they were married but hopeful. Sex, fun, and improvement. They had checked with their mother, who they and everyone else knew had a joyless marriage to an extreme sourpuss but who purported to be happy nonetheless in a resigned holy martyr way, and she had told them not to count on the first two. Improvement was possible.

Your marriage partner was supposed to make you better, strengthen your soul, send you on the path to salvation. You would do the same for him. And having their three reasons figured and written down in their separate journals, the sisters Duff were in a good position, they believed, to make a good choice.

But Gloria had only one choice, or if they were two choices, they were Richard or nobody. Richard was the only one taking up her time during her college days, and while she did love him, she wished for a choice. Babs had had Chuck and some guy whose name Gloria could no longer remember who had a speedboat and who proposed on their third date, but Babs chose Chuck who, as he laughingly put it, could not remember proposing. Rather, he explained, he was simply sucked into the path of Hurricane Babs, given the ride of his life. When Gloria said to her mother, only half complaining because she did love Richard, that a choice would be more interesting, her mother said no. "When a woman has a choice of two, she usually picks the wrong one."

So Gloria and Richard were married eleven months after Babs and Chuck because Gloria was eleven months younger than Babs, and the four wallowed in newly wed sex. *Wallowed* was Gloria's word and the other three found it apt, as if orgasms were food and relief and comfort all at once, as if fewer than two a day would cause rickets or iron-poor blood. They discussed it, the four of them, over martinis and gimlets in the evenings, and while they did not tell positions or points of entry, they marveled at how sex kept life laughable, how the bubbles of laughter were just under the surface always. "The colors are much brighter," Chuck said, "after a good roll in the hay."

And years later, Sheila Baker had pursed her prim lips and then said, "Thank God, we finished with that," making Babs roll her eyes and Gloria draw blood from the inside of her cheek.

※

Gloria and Babs went to the St. Louis Art Museum café after the funeral because they did not know the family well enough to go to the cemetery, and because it was just barely noon, too early for a beer and pretzels at some cozy corner bar. Beer in the early afternoon made the sisters sleepy.

"I'm supposed to stay gone all day," Babs said as she pulled out onto Grand Boulevard just barely before the funeral procession. "Chuck's painting the woodwork in Kelly's room while she's at the speech meet. He said what I can do to help is to stay gone."

"Richard's staring at the walls. I don't think he needs me for that," Gloria said. There was no way she knew to help him. "If someone would just tell me why it happened," he had said over and over, not finishing with a then what, though Gloria knew even if someone—she perhaps—could say why, there would be no resolution. But the falling flag pole was five months ago, in September, and his *if only* had died down, though the panicky look stayed in his eyes. He stared at the walls in panic as if they, too, would fall, as if he dared them to.

What had happened was called a freak accident by the newspapers whose reporters interviewed almost everyone concerned for four straight days. They spoke with Richard who as the school counselor was the one the children would turn to for answers. The wind that toppled the flag pole was called freak, too, but the children being in a straight, quiet line, ducks in a row, was not freakish. It was usual for the end of recess at Holy Cross grade school, especially for the third graders who always had lined up under the flagpole that crushed and killed four of the twenty-six immediately. Four died later in the hospital. Seven others were injured with assorted broken bones and concussions, and the eleven in the back of the line were unharmed physically.

Gloria had given every answer she knew to why: God's will, no reason, just chaos, we are not to know the purpose, *why* doesn't matter, talk to another counselor, don't dwell on it, don't forget freak and unexplained acts of goodness, and I agree that God is a big, mean bully.

"I know how you feel," she said. "I feel it also, to a lesser degree. Right here." She pressed her heart. "But life goes on."

"And on and on and on," he said. Once he had laughed bitterly as he said it. "Life goes on, but you look backwards."

She was a researcher for the St. Louis Genealogical Society. She tried to trace family names back as far as possible, discover when and why certain ancestors came to St. Louis. "I know what you mean," she said. "It's a pointless search. What difference does it make?"

"When you talk, I feel lonely," he said.

Improvement was one thing, she decided, but a wife could not do it all. He needed someone to be for him what Babs was for her, someone who could not stop loving him and someone he could not stop loving. She and Babs usually cried about Richard's pain, then plotted to bring him back to life, to get him to laugh again, to make him have fun.

They ordered shrimp salads at the café, and Gloria thought it a good sign that the shrimp were fresh. She realized later she should have counted the fifteen-minute wait as a bad omen, a portent. The trouble with signs was that when you noticed one, you missed another, and how could you tell.

"The shrimp reminds me of Mom," Babs said, and Gloria understood. She wanted to remember her mother in better days, but it was true. Fitzgibbons in Galveston, on the boardwalk. Fresh shrimp, right off the boats that pulled up in the small harbor even as they ate. Babs and Chuck and Gloria and Richard had taken

Mrs. Duff, Rowena, with them on their yearly joint vacation. Mr. Duff had been dead five years, and for three of them— after the first year of sorrow and adjustment—Rowena had been enjoying life possibly for the first time since her girlhood. The nine or so months before the Galveston trip, though, had been rife with confusion. For one thing, Richard had had to pick Rowena up for the usual Sunday morning bloodies because, as she kept forgetting Gloria's address, she was unable to make it on her own. And one morning, shortly before the Galveston excursion, she sat on the sofa in the sun, sipped her bloody with extra horseradish, and said "Am bee decks tor us. Am beeeee dicks tor us. Am beeee decks or rust. Am bee deck her just." She laughed when they said being able to use either hand, Mom. "Nice word," Chuck said. She laughed, but continued to say the syllables, sometimes mixing the order to "Am deck bee or us " until her head dropped back and she snored.

And Richard said lately he saw her face in his dreams, but not that one, the Galveston one. "It must be this war," he said. "The killing. I'm part of it by being who I am. You are, too. Our senators tumbled like so many dominoes lined up to make a pretty pattern."

"Yes," she said, and she meant it, too. She was part of it, but should she destroy her life by dwelling on it? And if she should suffer, if she deserved penance for her part in the war, what about those in charge? Her only crime had been in voting for them.

✳

"There is only so much a wife can do," she told Babs over the shrimp salad. "I cannot remake the world. I cannot stick my fingers in through his ears and rearrange the gray matter, disconnect one impulse, soften the edges so he can sleep through the war without seeing Mom's face."

"It's middle age," Babs said.

✳

"I don't fucking believe it," he said about Congress approving the war, and he had said the same about the flagpole as if belief were the key.

*

On the Saturday of Joe Baker's funeral, there were signs. The waiter at the art museum café forgot their water, though they asked for it twice. And when the shrimp salad was delivered, she and Babs both thought of their mother, the strong, intelligent woman who had always disliked farm subsidies and television news and hot rollers and Walt Disney movies. That woman who could run the bookmobile all day and plan a dinner party for the evening was gone by the time they dragged her to Galveston. In the restaurant in Galveston, just after their five platters of fresh shrimp salad and five frosty mugged beers arrived, Rowena Duff pushed back her chair and muttered "more, more, more." She spread her legs, letting her flowered skirt fall into the space between, and reached up under the flowers, swinging her arm back and forth, crying louder, "more, more, more." "More what, Mom?" Chuck asked. "Ketchup?" He laughed, but no one else did.

"Bay bees," she said. "Moremoremoremoremore!" She cried, her face crumpling like a ball of damp tissue paper.

"It was just us," Babs said, as if Rowena were talking sense, as if she had just forgotten. "Only two babies." But Rowena's cry became a wail before it ended, and they finally had to buy a round of drinks for the diners at the three closest tables, they felt so guilty at the outburst. Afterwards, Rowena slept quietly, her neck bent and her chin on her chest, as the four ate.

"Listen," Babs said as she sat in the art museum café across from her sister. "Richard will be fine. He's had some traumas. Life seems harder as we age. Harder and less sensible. Just keep him laughing, make him have fun."

"Someone took his sign down," Gloria said. "It was gone yesterday." The sign read "Stop the War in the Persian Gulf," a mild form of protest. Chuck had laughed at it, wondered if Richard expected someone to see it and tell the president, who would then exclaim What a good idea! and do it. But Gloria approved, even though she called it Richard's sign. So many people being killed for oil, he explained to her as if needing to justify his protest. But not our people: Iraqis and Kuwaitis who wore funny clothes. Some women wore veils as they went down. "He laughed at it being taken. He said Melissa, the new first grade teacher, had one that was set on fire. He said Melissa said something that causes such a reaction is essential."

"When we come over tonight, we'll do nothing but tell jokes. Kelly has a whole book of them." Babs pushed her tortoise-shell-framed glasses back up her nose. The two sisters looked alike— dark wavy hair, brown eyes, broad foreheads and wide chins, slightly upturned noses, smiles that showed as much gum as teeth, and a tendency toward fat, which they fought sporadically but successfully so far. And they were both nearsighted. Babs's ten-year-old, Kelly, looked like them, too, was clearly a Duff. Gloria had been startled recently when, as she was sitting across the kitchen table from Kelly, helping her with her fractions, Kelly had turned her young, rounded face up to the light and had revealed Gloria's father. It was as if his face were the foundation, the baby fat and youthful rosiness a disguise applied over it.

"It has been a long time since Richard really laughed," Gloria said. "I just remember the sound, so deep and reassuring. I can believe God is in his heaven when Richard laughs."

※

"You always want me to have fun," Richard said later as he sat beside Gloria on the couch, their arms touching. "I can't anymore. I can't have fun. I don't want to have fun. And don't think that after fifteen years you know me."

※

It was while planning the refreshments for the first school open house that Gloria and Babs worked with Sheila Baker. "Me and Joe've known each other since grade school. We fell in love when we were ten."

"Wonderful," Gloria had said because Sheila's statement seemed to call for acclaim.

"Yes, we've been through it all together," Sheila said. "Even all that nighttime stuff. Thank God neither of us cares about it anymore."

That was when Babs rolled her eyes at Gloria, and Gloria bit the inside of her cheek.

After lunch, Gloria and Babs went shopping. Gloria bought a black satin shower curtain, and Babs bought a few T-shirts for Kelly. They found a place in the mall to have a beer, watered-down, which Gloria later thought of as a bad sign, so it was almost four when Babs, her gas tank lower than empty, dropped Gloria off. Chuck and Babs were coming for happy hour at sixish, and then the four would decide where to eat. That was the usual Saturday.

Richard was not home when Gloria arrived, and there was no note. She hung the shower curtain, imagining his surprise. It belonged in a bordello, he would say, and they would laugh at it. It had red satin roses at the top where the hooks went through. She put a few glasses in the dishwasher, and other than that, her house was clean enough for Babs and Chuck. Richard would mix the whiskey sours at the last minute, so she had nothing else to do until it was time to change her clothes. She poured herself a glass of chablis and, as it was an unseasonably warm February Saturday, she put on a jacket and sat on the front porch, looking for Richard's car. "Are you having fun?" she often asked him, especially at parties when their paths would cross—they never mingled together—and he would say, "Don't I always?"

Because her ancestors had been too busy or too ignorant to keep good records, because some births were out of wedlock, because so many of her foremothers and fathers could not read or write, and because they—she imagined—had so deliberately yearned to be other than what they had been in a different country, and because even those who tried to retain parts of their customs were eventually swallowed by the great wave of America, she was rootless. She had not been able to trace her own genealogy beyond five generations on her mother's side, and four on her father's.

And would there have been any lessons in what an ancient believed or in how she had made her husband happy again? Her mother had been married to a man different from Richard in every way. Her father had fought his own demons of disappointment because he was human, not Irish or the Irish-Flemish-Spanish mixture she had discovered. Was there an Irish response to the Desert Storm invasion?

She hugged herself. Richard was her connection. Richard and Babs and Chuck and Kelly, family formed and reformed. Her parents were dead, her mother finally slipping away peacefully, so they liked to believe, more than a year ago. She was childless. There was no continuity, no chain for or through her. She was just a last link, dangling free.

At five-thirty she showered behind black satin, sorry Richard was not yet home so she could wrap the curtain around herself, expose pieces slowly as a tease.

At six-fifteen, Babs and Chuck showed up, joke book in hand, and Chuck mixed the whiskey sours, making them too sweet. By eight, the sweet whiskey sours had produced a dull thudding ache at the base of Gloria's skull. None of the jokes were funny. Chuck complained of being too hungry to wait much longer, but Gloria would not leave the house, so they ordered a pizza. "Richard'll hear about this," Chuck said. "We'll save the box for him, spread some canned sauce and a little salt on it."

"I think I'm eating the box," Babs said. "Did we order extra cardboard?"

No one laughed, and so the evening went. By nine-thirty, Gloria wanted to call the police, but Chuck said to wait. "Richard has been a little, you know, depressed. Maybe he just needs time alone. Maybe he went to the park and fell asleep under a tree. Maybe he tried to rush home, feeling guilty, but maybe he got tied up in a jam on Highway 55. Maybe he's turning the corner now. Wait, he's almost here. We'll hear his car any minute. Let's look." And they all stood behind the couch, looked out the front window.

At ten-thirty, Chuck was snoring in the winged chair, his face pressed into an upholstered corner. Babs was on martinis and, with her shoes off, was sitting cross-legged on the couch. "When we were kids," she said, "you got everything I fought for. The oldest has it so much harder." Her voice was teary. "I didn't want to be one of the sisters Duff. I just wanted to be me—Babs. My first year at college I pretended I was an only child. The next year you showed up, and we were a team."

"Grow up," Gloria said. She heard this every time Babs drank too much. "Tell me something new."

"The sisters Duff. We may as well have been Siamese twins."

"That's Thailand by now," Chuck said, his eyes still closed, his face still pressed into the corner.

"You loved it," Gloria said.

"Go back to sleep," Babs said to Chuck.

By midnight, Babs and Gloria were hugging each other, crying over the fear they'd lived in of their father's anger, recalling hiding in the pantry, running up to the school yard and staying all day. "Mom never even flinched when he yelled," Gloria said. "It made him try harder."

At 1 A.M. Gloria called the police, and the woman on the end of the line was rude. "Did you have a fight? . . . You don't know what he was wearing? . . . Describe the car. You don't know the year?" Gloria just knew it was an '80 something, the mid-eighties. It was a blue Ford. Ordinarily, Gloria would have taken it as a bad sign, the woman's rudeness, but it was too late for signs. It was all bad anyway, everything was bad. Richard was in a ditch, in a coma, in heaven.

He entered as soon as she hung up. Chuck sat up and began teasing about the cardboard pizza, but Richard said he had to talk to Gloria alone. Would they please leave? He said he was sorry about dinner and a lot more. He patted both Babs and Chuck on the backs as they left, saying they were good sorts.

As soon as they were alone, even before Chuck's car had warmed up, he came out with it. Melissa. He was going to marry her, as soon as he and Gloria were divorced, of course. "You make me have fun," he said. "You've made me have fun for fifteen years. I'm trapped like your mother was by your idea of fun. It's all falling apart."

"What?" She told herself not to believe what he said.

"*All* I said. The world. Civilization. Us. Me."

"I know," she said, placing a hand on his arm, pulling him to the couch. "I feel it, too." It's not true. None of this is true. "You need a break. Stop thinking. Take a vacation from yourself."

"Melissa doesn't try to cheer me up. She doesn't try to argue me out of it. She doesn't give me cliché answers." He paused. "I don't want to talk just about Melissa. I know you're hurt."

Genius, she thought in spite of herself. Genius, she thought with hate.

He was sitting beside her, patting her arm. "I don't want to be happy. I don't want to laugh. I don't want to be improved."

She remained on the couch as he went to the bedroom and packed a bag, a small one with enough for one or two nights at the most. Even when he went for his toothbrush he did not seem to notice the shower curtain. "Have you ever thought," he said as he stood by the door, overnight bag in hand, "that the beauty of loving someone is that he is *not* you? Not an extension? Melissa says we are all alone. None of us really knows the other, or ever can."

"Bye," she said as she stood at the window and watched his car pull away. I don't believe it. It's not true. Then she paced the living and dining room a while, thirty minutes or longer, wondering at the cause, going back over the day that began with a funeral, though knowing the day was not it at all.

She used her key and let herself in quietly, careful not to think of much but her actions of tiptoeing across Babs's living room, of taking a blanket from the hall closet, of changing into her Chinese silk pajamas. Just as she closed her eyes, she thought it was a good thing she and Richard had not had children. Then she thought it would all work out later. Richard was under a lot of strain. She understood. She knew exactly what he was going through. His blaming it on her was proof of his confusion. Imagine not wanting to laugh.

She didn't know who first discovered her, but she awoke facing the light blue dacron of the couch, aware that others were tiptoeing by, whispering when they were near. Kelly stood over her for a while, watching for signs of life, she guessed. She drifted back to sleep, and when she awoke again, she faced out toward the room. It was afternoon. The sunlight fell directly on the patch of carpet beside the couch. She closed her eyes when she heard Babs coming. She kept her eyes closed as Babs knelt beside her, brushed her hair from her forehead, smoothed her brow with a cool hand. "Poor baby sister," Babs said. "Playing possum."

If only Richard had a brother. Or even a sister.

During dinner, the family sat around the dining room table, but listened to the news report from the television in the living room. Gloria could have watched upside down had she opened her eyes and tilted her head back. Instead she listened from her position on the couch, still pretending to be asleep. She did not yet want to say what was wrong, knew it would be more final if she told someone else. So with her eyes closed, she heard of the victory. Only one hundred hours of ground war. The Gulf War, Desert Storm, whatever the president called it, was over. She rolled over and sighed. She did not know if victory was a good sign or not.

On Iron Street

M uscles and flab and bones and skin and curves and planes, light and shadow, the dry and the damp— Kate Tucker wanted it all. She twisted her wedding ring around her thin finger. Her hands were cold and her ring was even looser than usual. "Would you do me a teeny tiny favor?" she asked Carl, her husband.

"Of course," he said, boomed as he did when he wanted to seem happy, a mannerism left over from his days on the road. He feared her twisting her ring and not looking at him. He would be pleased to do her a favor, teeny tiny or gigantic, either one.

"Take your clothes off," she said. "Sit on the edge of the tub." She looked up at him then, her eyes sparkling. They were as blue as the sky on a fall afternoon, horizon blue he had called them when he courted her, a somewhat lighter, hazier blue than the sky straight above, but a blue that promised more than a man could see. That was how he talked to her all those years ago. After thirty-three years, her eyes no longer took his breath away.

"I'm not at my best in my birthday suit," he said. "Haven't you noticed? Why not go the other way? I'll put on the old tux, suck in my gut. I'd be a pretty picture then."

"You thwart me because you hate me." She turned her face, and he prepared for tears. He sat beside her on the couch then, wrapped her in his arms, held her so her head was under his chin, but he did not squeeze. She was fragile, had always been fragile.

"Hey," he said. "It's okay. I'll pose. You can capture me in all my natural born glory." Her sobs shook him. "You know I always say yes. I have for thirty-three years." She nodded. Her hair was stiff, and it scratched his chin. "Can we wait until after dinner, though? And after I've had a few drinks for warmth?"

She jumped up so abruptly he bit his tongue. "I knew you'd put it off." Her complexion was blotchy, a portent of a troubled night.

"Okay," he said. "Now. We'll do it right now." He slipped his loafers off. "See this? I'll strip right now."

"No. Later," she said, her tears already drying on her cheeks. "And don't worry about that old body. Get over your vanity. My teacher says one model he uses even has a hump on his back. And I have to learn to draw fat, too." She smiled suddenly, said she would take a hot bath before dinner, asked would he be so kind as to call her when dinner was ready.

He watched her glide down the hallway. Not just fragile, but high strung, delicate yet volatile. Her own mother had used all those words to describe her years ago when Carl, at twenty-eight, was dating the mother, just six years his senior. It had not been a romance, but rather the kind of dating a man and a woman who shared friends did. She, Kate's mother, had had a troubled adolescence and a seventeen-year-old daughter as a reminder, and almost immediately, Carl fell for the daughter, lovely and sad-looking. The Lady of Shalott, Rapunzel. He wanted to protect her. Kate was eighteen when they married and nineteen when Tony was born. She was only twenty-three when she locked Tony in the closet, and the community college Saturday morning figure drawing class she had missed this morning was merely the latest in a string of activities meant to keep her from sliding back into the depression she danced on the edge of, at least one foot always crossing the line. Carl pictured her that way, imagined his job was to grab the other foot, hold on.

Kate sank down into the tub, the water as hot as she could stand it, hot enough to turn her skin bright red, make it sting. *He knows I take my pills. He counts them everyday. Yet still he watches. He won't accept that I'm mean and cruel. Was born that way. I ruined my son, my only son, a beautiful boy I loved, my*

reward and grand prize for letting my mother's boyfriend claim me, touch me. I am mean. I am more than crazy. But he looks for signs, after all this time not sure what I am. She smiled. She enjoyed acting crazy for him. She moved her legs to make waves and thought about those questions the psychiatrists had asked her. Never once did they ask the right question. Did she love Tony and Carl? Yes, she had answered each time, though she had known she could just as easily have said no. It all depended on how she looked at it, at them. And she loved Tony better when he was in the closet. He was easier to love that way. Was she sorry? Of course, but that was not it. No one ever asked her if she was mean. Yes, she would have said. Look what I've done. Look at what I still do. She smiled again. She took credit for the lines etched deeply in Carl's forehead.

In the same four-family apartment building on Iron Street in South St. Louis, in the apartment above the Tuckers', Jay and Cecilia Patterson were dressing for a night out. They were young, recently married, and members of a large group of other couples who had weekend parties. This Saturday, they were going to one couple's new home, and as Cecilia was tucking her man-tailored chambray shirt into her jeans, she asked Jay where this new home was.

"Somewhere west," he said. "Past Highway 270." He brushed his thick, fur-brown hair and smiled at himself in the bathroom mirror.

She stood behind him to brush her hair, ducking and standing on tiptoe to see around him. Not that it mattered. She doubted she was going to the party. "Where west of 270?" She had seen him *not* take directions over the phone two nights ago. "Yes," he had said into the receiver. "Sure. Okay." He had not written anything down, but had smirked at her, sneered at the guy on the other end. He often called the guy on the other end, the male half of the couple, cocky. Now they would be hopelessly lost. That is, if they went at all.

"Somewhere in some fakely elegant subdivision. Somewhere ostentatious. You can count on that." He smirked at himself in the mirror, then winked. When he was ten, he had crashed his bicycle, skidded face down onto a gravel shoulder, and come up with two chips of brown rock embedded in his upper lip. His mother had decided the rocks would be impossible to remove, and so simply dabbed Bactine on his face and sent him back out to play. Fourteen years later, the chips were still firmly in place, giving him a crooked mouth, a diagonal smile that most women called cute. The gravel had become part of his charm. Lately, Cecilia thought it the sum of his charm.

"You don't know, do you? We'll be lost." His new secretary had called twice last week. Jay's explanation was that she had been going over his appointment calendar, but he lowered his voice when he spoke to her, turned his back on Cecilia. "We'll have to call, say we lost the directions."

"We're not calling," he said.

"*I'm* calling." She pointed to herself. She was as sure of their affair as if she had caught them in bed. Her stomach was full of needles, had been for a few days; it hurt no matter how she moved. She raised her voice. "*I* am calling." When he did not turn from the mirror, did not look at her, she walked down the hall to the dining area where the phone hung on the wall. She picked it up and dialed information for the new number. He was beside her.

"No," he said. "We're not calling."

"Jerk," she said. If she killed him, it would be self-defense. He was ruining her health. She spoke to the Southwestern Bell assistant, but before she could finish her request, he grabbed the receiver and banged it down on its holder. "Cheater," she said, swinging at him, catching him on the edge of his chin as he leaned back. "Cheater. Get lost by yourself."

She grabbed her purse and ran to the front door. "Don't be foolish," he said, but she slammed the door on his words. While running down the stairs, she almost pushed a woman carrying a toddler out of her way. Cecilia did not apologize, just dodged to the side and kept going. There was a fire inside her chest. She could picture it—red and yellow flames reaching up her throat. She had expected the fight, but her rage was shocking. She had not known such anger until Jay. As she yanked open the outside door, she cursed herself for forgetting her coat. Damn me, damn February, damn him, damn his secretary, damn me. The litany of damns filled her, stayed with her all the way across the parking lot to her car.

✳

"Is Uncle Joe an angel?" the toddler asked its mother.

✳

Kate was still soaking when she heard the upstairs door slam, heard Cecilia run down the stairs. Idiot, Kate thought. I could teach her a thing or two about getting attention. You have to do more than slam a few doors.

✳

June Currie, downstairs in Apartment B, across from Kate, also heard the slamming and running. June was practicing going forward and backing up in her new motorized wheelchair. There was an on/off switch on the left arm and a stick that controlled speed and direction on the right arm. June could back down her hallway faster than a whole person could have walked it forwards. When she turned into the living room, though, she just barely caught the corner of the couch. She backed up again, took a full-speed run down the hall, switched to forward, and moved up as quickly as possible, the chair humming. At the end table, she started her right turn, holding the stick steady, and turning cleanly into the living room. She missed the couch, but did not release the stick quickly enough, and ended up facing the sliding glass doors to the concrete slab patio rather than her writing desk and computer. She pushed the stick down and made a quarter turn, all the while plotting the story of a flight attendant who is invited to a captain's party that turns into an orgy.

The flight attendant gets cold feet and runs out in her underwear, only to be arrested by St. Louis cops for indecent exposure and taken into the station where she is booked and, still in her underwear, questioned by the two men. The flight attendant's underwear is a white silky camisole and a pair of edible bikini panties, mostly spun sugar, that starts to melt as she talks. June would call it "The Station's Taffy Pull," or "Sugar for the Men in Blue." She published as Ranger Rick, Harry True Man, Piglet, Mr. Softee, and the one she would use for this story, Lola Lash. She would send this one to *Men's World* where it would take up space between the pictures. She needed to send a story off soon; the payments on the new wheelchair would take almost half of her savings.

Cecilia may teach at the new South County High School, but Jay knew he was really the teacher. He thought that after he went out for a twelve-pack of Budweiser and then fixed the apartment so she could not get back in. He was teaching her to fight. Not that she would win; he was unbeatable, and she would learn that, too. But she was getting better, more creative. Like with her notes. "Jay Patterson is a selfish liar who uses others," was the unoriginal first one. She had stuck it in his back pocket when she patted his butt as he left the apartment one morning. That alone had been clever, he was pleased to admit. She had been angry because he had not gone to the new school open house and faculty reception with her. The note had fallen out at Mario's Italian Village when he reached for his wallet. The second note was better: "Jay Patterson should have his intestines ripped out, tied into a noose, and used to hang him with." That one was inside his appointment book, and was because he had not gone to the high school's Winter Wonderland Dance with her last week, had not helped chaperon with other young teachers and their spouses.

Emotions were healthy. Anger was good. She was too re-pressed. He thought about her and smiled as he removed the plastic cover from the bell part of the doorbell. It was good that she learned to fight. He cut up a dust rag—once a pair of his briefs—and stuffed it around the bell striker. Now he was teaching her that when she fought with him, she would always lose.

How Cecilia knew about his secretary was a mystery, but it had been nothing other than a lunchtime diversion. And it was Cecilia's fault. His secretary had seen both notes, and he had had to unburden himself, had had to admit he was no good at intimate, trusting relationships. He confessed that he acted like an asshole, often on purpose. He even said he hated himself for it. The secretary, who had taken the same required psych courses in college as he had, said his need to control, to withhold love, came from his childhood. Surely his parents had neglected him. Or else they had been too watchful. She could not remember which, but either way, she knew he was a victim, not a villain.

Jay unplugged the phone and bolted the front and only door. Sure, Cecilia may bang on the door for a while, but her hand would hurt more than his ears. She had said once that his meanness came from parents who gave him lots of attention, but the wrong kind. Seldom unconditional love. She was determined to give him the unconditional love he had missed. He sat on the couch, opened his second beer, and pulled a slip of paper out of his shirt pocket. It was the directions he had called for yesterday from work. Cecilia would have to learn not to believe him.

✳

June was typing "Sugar for the Men in Blue" when she heard another door slam upstairs, this one on the Bakers' apartment directly overhead. A funeral party was in progress up there, and just the two words together, funeral and party, reminded June of her mother's line: "When your dad cashes in his chips, I'll have one party after another." June often recalled her mother's words, though the two women had not spoken for twenty-five years. Her dad may have cashed in his chips by now. If so, June hoped he had gone out a winner.

Well, the old produce man upstairs was dead, but June had not known him, hardly knew his name. She had been in Apartment B less than a year, had moved in right before they cut her left leg off above the knee, making a first-floor place with an outside ramp a necessity. If only you had been diagnosed sooner, the doctors said, we could have saved your leg. "I don't care," she told each one, as well as the nurses and aides. "I'm sedentary. I don't like to move anyway. Never have." She knew she disgusted them, all two hundred pounds of her, and that two hundred was without the leg. An editor at *Men's World* had once asked for a photo of

Lola Lash, but June had refused, explaining that a horrible fire had disfigured her, ravished her loveliness. It was more romantic than admitting she was a fat woman who wore mail-order tent dresses and gave herself monthly crew cuts. She left the hospital minus a leg but with four completed stories in her notebook: "The Night Nurse," "The Orderly's Specialty," "Who Was behind that Mask?" and "Love Surgery." They covered the down payment on her wheelchair.

"You should count your blessings," a motherly nurse had said before June's discharge. "You're right," June answered. She played with her television controls to keep from laughing. The motherly nurse, gooey brown cow eyes and all, was a main character in a fifth story June was just beginning. In it, the nurse wore a studded leather bra and a leather thong under her uniform. The leather was as brown as her cow's eyes. "How Now Brown Cow" would be about the hospital chaplain's greatest temptation.

"Losing a leg is nothing compared to what Jesus suffered. As long as you still have all your friends and family and job and your good mind, you'll be fine. Think of that."

No friends, family, or job, but you are right, June thought. The mind is good. Always has been. Is not trapped within the body, either, not restricted by.

"You're too young to give up on life," the brown-eyed nurse said.

"Right." June laughed in spite of herself. She had never given up. Just because at forty-four she was an obese diabetic virgin with one leg and no friends and parents she had left behind in Minnesota twenty-five years earlier, did not mean she did not live or want to. She made money from the stories she wrote, and had an awfully good time as well. She often reread her favorites, laughing and marveling at the sogginess of sex. It was all damp and wet and moist and slippery and slick and juicy. Not that she cared about accuracy, but never having tried it, not even with herself, she wondered if it truly was that way. She wrote one story about aphrodisiacs in the water supply of a small town in which the unprecedented amount of sexual activity in the town raised the humidity level by 5 percent.

"He was a prince," one of the funeral revelers called back on his way down the stairs. "A real prince." The prince of produce, June thought, immediately plotting a story in which cucumbers and carrots played a major role.

✳

Carl heard Joe Baker referred to as a prince and felt guilty for staying downstairs. Surely though, Sheila Baker, the widow, would understand Kate's instability, would know his first duty was to his wife. Kate was upset enough that she had had to miss her art class for the funeral mass. Now he would pay by posing nude for her. He always paid, even for what he did not do, like with Tony. He was sure he paid more than Kate.

The evening he came home from Jonesville, he had started paying. "Anything exciting happen while I was gone?" he asked as he had each Friday for five years.

"Yes," Kate said. She wore an off-the-shoulder peasant blouse tucked into tight white jeans. Her blond curls bounced on her shoulders, her horizon blue eyes sparkled, and her face was flushed with excitement. "You'll want to hear this." She sat on his lap. "They've taken Tony. It's finally over."

The closet had been her way of coping with a four-year-old. She had locked him in for a few hours at first, then for most of the day, then a day and a night, then two days at a time. On one of his rare release times, Tony told two women in the laundry room of the apartment building they lived in then. The women believed the small blond boy because he asked them for help. And he said please. "Please help me," had been his first words to them.

When Kate was questioned, she freely admitted her guilt. She said Tony should live somewhere else. It had all happened on Thursday, and Kate refused to tell anyone how to contact Carl because she knew he would be home soon. Besides, she said to her mother and the Child Welfare people, the ones she said later had dull but official little heads they constantly shook, it really was none of Carl's business.

When Carl was allowed to see Tony, he asked the obvious. "Why didn't you tell *me*? Why didn't you ask *me* for help?" Tony shrugged, looked older than four. "You were busy," he said.

Carl gave up traveling almost immediately, took a desk job with MaidFresh, and Tony was eventually given to Kate's mother, who kept him for four years until all concerned decided Kate's treatment was successful. After Tony came back, Kate seemed the loving mother, dressing up for parents' night at school, helping Tony with his math homework, baking cookies for after-school treats. Tony grew to be a shy, friendless, almost invisible boy, and Kate's medication gave her recurring kidney infections. Still, they made it, Carl told himself. *He* guided them through their troubles, like a sheep dog guiding his lost lambs, running in circles so they moved out of danger. Or, he thought, like a puppeteer, he pulled their strings at the right times, made them turn their heads and close their blank eyes to worries. He did it for ten years until Tony left for a California college.

Tony had not been back home since. For fourteen years, his infrequent phone calls had been pleasant enough, though full of pauses and *well*s. "I guess I'll let you go," he said to end each one, and he often said, "I'll have to plan a trip to St. Louis soon," though all three of them knew he would not. And he was careful not to invite them to California, to even suggest a visit.

But Carl imagined dropping in uninvited, by himself, chatting as he had done with his customers in those lost days, sharing stories of golf scores over beers, perhaps discussing their cars or laughing ruefully about an ascendent politician. Tony would tease Carl about his expanding waistline. Carl would pat his son's back, say, "Don't do anything I wouldn't do," before he left.

Carl checked on Kate in the tub. "Don't get waterlogged," he called through the door.

"Glug glug," she said and laughed when he tried the knob.

"You shouldn't lock yourself in," he said.

✳

He was getting old, old and dull. Twenty-eight years ago, she had told him being locked in a closet had not seemed so bad to her. "It was either Tony or me," she said. "I wanted to be the one in the closet, but I had too much to do." He had stared at her, his mouth open. He had started to age right then, right before her eyes. He had no imagination. "For five days a week, I was just a picture in your wallet," she said to him during their first week of therapy. "I was captured in plastic."

＊

Carl went back to the living room and turned on the television. Relax, he told himself. She's taking her pills. He wished there was something funny on. No one made funny shows anymore. He heard another mourner call out, "Let me know what you need," and felt guilty again. Joe had always seemed sneaky, but his widow was kind. Though she had never met Tony, she asked about him often, worried that he was in each reported California quake. Still, Carl could not leave Kate home alone. And here was another annoyance. Something was causing interference on his set. All he could get, on any channel, was a black screen with white dots flashing across it.

＊

"We just weren't ready," the widow said to a departing cousin. "He always wanted to pick out his own casket, plan the service ahead. We just weren't ready. That's the thing."

＊

Downstairs, June was inventing dialog as she practiced quick right angle turns. "Should we check her for concealed weapons?" one cop asked the other as the flight attendant stood before them in edible bikinis. "Rules are rules," the second cop said. Or maybe he added, "you can't judge a suspect by appearances." June laughed. One of the three characters in her scene should blush. Readers liked a little blushing. She made a sharp right turn into the kitchen and caught the oven door handle, so she quickly backed up and tried gain. Her chair buzzed and whined.

＊

Cecilia cooed to her pair of Victoria Crowned pigeons as she entered the rudely constructed aviary. It was a four-by-eight pen of two-by-fours and chicken wire, twelve feet high. Various shelves and branches for roosts were built into the end protected by a partial roof. The advertising coo of the Victoria Crowned pigeon was like a series of prolonged moos, the sound made by blowing across an empty bottle. Cecilia imitated it. The pair and the aviary out behind her parents' garage had been an engagement gift to her alone from her father. "Trust me," he had said to her bewildered look. "Pigeons are relaxing. They form devoted couples. They let you control them." Her pair had beautiful blue and gray crests, like the headdresses Indian chiefs wore in old westerns, spiky and brilliant. Their names were Cecilia and Jay—they had been an engagement gift after all—and though her father had primary care of them, she visited a few times a week, not only when her rage at Jay drove her out.

She had stopped on the way and bought a plastic bag of dried banana slices. She offered banana slices to them, held her hand out to them, and, as usual, the male let the female eat first. Cecilia had read that was standard pigeon behavior, so she assumed it was what happened, assumed the one sitting on the egg and eating first was the female. In fact, both birds were gloriously marked, one as bright as the other. Both were large, and both bowed and strutted for admiration.

"Here, Jay," Cecilia said to the male, and he cooed at her, but would have cooed at any sound she made. Pigeons did not recognize their names, and she didn't think she would bother to name whatever popped out of the egg.

She had noticed the egg a week ago, and one reason she guessed the one sitting on the egg was the female was that it was eight-thirty. The female took her turn incubating after dusk. Both pigeons kept up the nodding and cooing while she was there. The male even imitated a parrot and perched on her shoulder, though not when she called him, getting a foot temporarily tangled in her hair. After about half an hour, she left the love birds and knocked on her parents' back door.

"How're the birds?" her father asked.

"Fine," she said. "Happy."

"And how are you?" her mother asked.

"Fine," she said. "Just fine. Jay's fine, too."

"Where's your coat?" her mother asked.

"I don't need it. I'm not cold."

✳

By nine-thirty, only close family members and even closer friends remained at the funeral party. Most of the food was gone, and someone suggested calling out for pizzas. The widow wished they would never go home. She wanted to say, "Why don't you all move in?"

✳

Downstairs in Apartment B, June was finishing her flight attendant story. All she had to do was run the spell check and print. She would get two hundred for this one, and she had churned it out in less than three hours. When she finished, she would take a break, eat a frozen enchilada dinner, and maybe write the produce story later. She knew she would eventually write one involving a motorized wheelchair, maybe on Monday. She would call it "Lust on Wheels," borrowing her mother's favorite criticism. "He thinks he's just sex on wheels," her mother would say of a neighbor, or "She thinks she's just *it* on wheels," for an aunt or for one of June's classmates. She once told June, "You better watch out. All you'll be is fat. Fat on wheels." June smiled. Imagine her mother finally getting something right.

✳

Jay finished his twelve-pack by ten-thirty. Three and a half hours, he wrote down on the back of the directions to the party. Two hundred and ten minutes. He divided it by twelve. That would be one beer every seventeen and a half minutes. He did the figuring to beat Cecilia to it. He called it irrigating his brain cells. It was drought relief. Besides, Cecilia was visiting her birds. He knew her pattern. Those stupid birds. She would end up giving them both histoplasmosis. Anyway, she could sleep with the birds for all he cared. She wouldn't get in, and what was better, she wouldn't disturb him in the process of not getting in. The doorbell was muffled, the phone unplugged. He turned off the television, which had been almost worthless all night because of some odd interference, and went into the bedroom, closing the door behind him to muffle her knocks even more. Unconditional love was a myth, bullshit. Everything had conditions. Why should love be different? As soon as he closed his eyes, he was running uphill on legs made of limp water balloons. He breathed hard with the effort.

✳

At eleven, Kate said, "It's time. You said you'd do it." Her bottom lip protruded slightly and her eyes narrowed. "I know you'll weasel out of it."

"Turn up the heat," he said. I've arranged my whole life for you, he thought. If I were the weaseling out kind, I'd be gone. He gulped his brandy. Long gone. "Let's try to get the bathroom a bit warmer." I'd be in California with the son I let you ruin were I the weaseling out kind. "In about ten minutes I'll brave it," he said as she spun the thermostat dial dramatically and the blower motor revved up.

✳

When Cecilia pulled into the small parking lot behind the four-family on Iron Street, she saw Jay's car in its usual spot, and she noticed her upstairs apartment was dark. He had not waited up, had not even left a light on. He could learn a thing or two from a male pigeon.

Fifteen minutes later, after banging on the door, trying the quiet doorbell, standing in the parking lot and throwing gravel at their bedroom window but missing most of the time, she felt the white hot flames burning her from the inside again. The scum, the stupid, sleazy, lousy, rotten-brained, small-minded, black-hearted, lily-livered, weak-kneed, gravel-lipped, low-life bastard. He would not win. Not this one. She would get into her own by-God apartment if she had to chisel out the bricks one by one.

She knew there was a ladder in the basement storeroom. She had seen it once as she explored the basement, killing time waiting for her clothes to dry. Tonight, the storeroom was unlocked as before, and as she entered it, she saw just the end of a ladder sticking out behind large windows and screens. To move the screens, she had to first move two large boxes of carpet samples, a tool box, and a wooden chest that seemed full of scrap metal. She would use the ladder to go in a window, and she considered her choices as she moved the carpet samples. The bathroom window was too small, and one of the front windows may attract a vigilant neighbor or police attention. But if she went in their bedroom window, he may hear her coming, lock the window before she could climb the ladder. By the time she had moved the windows, had leaned them against another wall, half expecting a crash, she was shaking all the way down to her veins. Not from exertion, from anger. And if the windows she had moved slipped and shattered into a billion shards, she would pay. It would be worth buying new windows for the whole damn building to prove to Jay Dickhead upstairs that he was not always the winner. And then she knew her plan. He was not smart enough to have locked the sliding glass door to the balcony. He would never think she'd use a ladder.

The ladder was a fourteen footer, all in one piece, made of wood, and heavier than she had known ladders could be. It took her ten minutes to drag it across the floor and out of the storeroom and across the laundry room to the bottom of the stairs. She had been in the basement twenty-five minutes all together.

She knew she could not lift and carry the ladder, so she would have to drag it up the stairs. She would pace herself, rest often. This was not a race. Just so she got in before morning when he awoke and deigned to unlock the door, just so she could beat him and take some of the swagger from his walk. As she dragged the ladder, it banged against her shins and she cursed at the pain, imagining the purple patches she would have to hide under slacks all next week. The ladder also banged against the stairs and the wall enclosing the stairs. When she got to the top of the stairs, she used her left foot to prop open the basement door as she worked the long ladder up and out, and the ladder bounced against the foot, bruising her toes. Perspiration ran into her eyes. Luckily it was a straight shot to the back door leading to the parking lot, but she had to prop that door open as well. She leaned the ladder against the stairway wall before she went out to search for a prop. When she returned with one of the cobblestones the landlord had set in a square around a bed of dormant daisies, she noticed the ladder had slid back a few feet.

✳

June Currie heard noises coming from the storeroom directly below her living room and was intrigued. According to the fine print on her lease agreement, the storeroom was off limits, so June parked at her door, waiting to see what was going on. If it was a burglary, she wanted it to work. She paid the landlord twenty dollars a month more than the others did just for washer/dryer hookups and used appliances in her first floor apartment. Now the decrepit washer he supplied her with was refusing to rinse, and he had been merely promising to fix it for a week. He deserved a break-in. Besides, she could use the crime in a story. Some of her magazines wanted thieves and drug runners woven into the sex. One with a higher class readership preferred embezzlers and junk bond traders capable of multiple orgasms.

So June's door was opened a crack, and she watched Cecilia drag the wooden ladder outside. It was not what she expected, but not bad. Surely she could make a quick soggy story out of it. It grew more interesting when the new widow upstairs opened her door and called out, "Is that you, Joe?"

"It's Cecilia," the young woman said. "Your neighbor. Sorry to disturb you."

"Don't worry, dear," the new widow called down. "I'm going to be disturbed for quite a while."

Carl was posed on the edge of the tub and Kate sat on the toilet, facing him. She had been making a few tentative pencil lines on her newsprint page, but that was all she could do and she knew it, knew it as an old friend, the defeat. She had lived with it for fifty-one years; she could taste its metallic bitterness; she could feel it dissolve her heart. Mean people were not allowed to succeed. Maybe that was fair, and more than fair: it was proof she was what she knew she was. The gods recognized her, no matter how she smiled. They would allow her no talent for drawing just as they allowed her no talent for upholstery or filmmaking or jazz dancing or piano playing or debating or any of the other outlets she had tried, each time with diminished hope, wanting to succeed at at least one activity before her death.

And as she looked at Carl, clearly an old man, she understood death better than ever. It was on its way. True, he was only sixty-two, but his chest hairs were white, and his chest had a hollow in it, right between his ever more apparent breasts. His stomach area was not exactly overlarge but was flabby and ill-defined. The gentle slope began under his arms and continued to where his legs bent as he sat on the edge of the tub. His legs were thin, yet still he had held them together at first. "Open up," she said. "The penis and scrotum are what I want." And he had opened his legs, giving her a good view of his deflated looking scrotum, more yellow than pink, and covered with a few wiry white hairs like an inexpertly plucked chicken. And his penis, curled and small. "Like a hand grenade," he had joked once when they were newly married. "It's about the right size, has lines and creases all over it, and can go off suddenly." She remembered it now, his joke, and remembered laughing at it all those years ago, still so new at marriage that she tried to be what he wanted.

She posed him so his arms were hanging at his side, and though he slumped and looked as though his sliding off the edge of the tub was imminent, she made him keep his chin up. He looked hopelessly defiant. Or, she thought, pathetic. Of course, it was she. She had placed him in that position. She was the pathetic one, she knew. That went without saying. Crazy and mean and pathetic. But looking at him, trying to capture him on paper which she knew she could not do, she wondered. Is this what I've been afraid of losing for so long?

✳

When all fourteen feet of the ladder were outside, Cecilia rested. She looked up at her dark apartment. Male and female pigeons took turns incubating the egg, and their schedules, at least in captivity, were regular. The male's turn was from approximately 9 A.M. until dusk. He did it so she could walk around, try a different view, eat more. Was that love? Were the birds capable of what Jay was not?

✳

He was not sure who or what was after him, but he knew malevolence was just a breath or two away. He knew he would fail because his damned legs were moving in slow motion; he was actually moving backwards. If only he could wake up.

Cecilia managed to drag the ladder under her balcony, but found standing it up was impossible. It was too heavy. She did get it pointed almost straight up twice, but still it leaned too much, tipped back over on her like in a slapstick routine. She had three splinters in her right hand by the time she admitted she needed help. But who? Not her father or any of her and Jay's group of friends. They would only disapprove of her efforts, of Jay, of their marriage. It must be someone she could lie to. The crippled lady who barely said hi, who seemed shy yet spooky, had been watching her. Cecilia had noticed her front door opened a crack. But what good would a cripple be? And Sheila Baker lived alone now. Last week, Cecilia would have asked Joe, the produce man who had touched her hair five days ago when they met on the stairs. "Are you a true redhead?" he had asked.

When the doorbell sounded, Carl was asking himself the same old question, one he never answered because the question alone was frightening: why had he allowed Kate to ruin his life? Ruin was the word he rebelled against, but tonight he let it stay in his mind. Ruin. Because of Kate, he had lost his son, lost a good woman in her mother (his memory fooled him over the years, made him remember a passion that had not existed), and lost the only fun he could have had in a job. The desk was not his place. He was not funny there. He was not teased, not welcomed, not flattered, not anticipated as he had been when he called on department stores and sold MaidFresh sheets and towels, took orders really because the product sold itself. He had been invited into their homes, to their country clubs, had treated them to dinners at the best steak houses in town, showed them photos of his wife and child. "Lovely," they said about Kate. "How big he's getting," they said about Tony. "Just like his old man," Carl would joke. At the office, he was just old Carl who came in every day, old Carl who had a disturbed wife and a distant son and thus the forehead lines and the circles under his eyes. He was Carl who often could not even go out to lunch with his coworkers because Kate called exactly at lunchtime and accused him of hating her, required reassurances right then. The middle-aged woman with the dead eyes and stiff hair, the one before him with no talent and no ideas and little or no humanity, was his wife. Why had he ruined his life for her?

"It's the door," she said. "Let's ignore it."

He sighed. Normally he would agree to keep her as peaceful as possible, to avoid whatever intrusion of the outside world it would be, and thus avoid any new problems. As peaceful as possible. It was all he ever hoped for. It described the best of times. "What nonsense," he said. "I'll get it." He put on his maroon terry cloth robe and matching corduroy slippers, and went to the door. It was probably Sheila Baker asking to borrow something useless, he thought, because what she really wanted she could no longer have.

Instead, the young girl who lived upstairs smiled at him. Cecilia. He remembered her from the one evening last spring they had asked her and her husband down. It had been in late May, and some hope or scent in the air had made Kate want company. The crippled woman had just moved in across the hall, but so had the new young couple upstairs, and they promised to be more cheery. Carl remembered that she taught high school and that she was capable of shrugging off the hateful remarks her husband made. The husband had said he admired career women, and then had excluded his wife. "I mean those in a man's world," he'd said. "Those who compete with men, with me. Teaching has always been for women." Cecilia had shrugged, then smiled, just as she was doing now.

"I've locked myself out," she said. "My husband is out of town, and I have to get in. I'm sure my balcony door is unlocked, and I just need your help for a few minutes. I have to get the ladder up to the balcony."

"I don't have a ladder," he said. "But come in." He was about to tell her to spend the night with them, then call a locksmith in the morning, but he remembered she had family in town. Such an invitation would surely be denied, perhaps even suspect. He and

Kate, though all right for a few moments' help, were not a known commodity, may be perverts. And, he admitted, they were—just not the typical kind.

"I have a ladder outside. It's from the basement."

"That old monstrosity?" He marveled as he changed into his jeans. How had she done it? Anyway, it was a relief. He looked much younger in jeans. When they went out the door, he noticed the one across the hall was ajar. As always. The poor thing just hid behind her door and saw life through a crack. If Kate were up to it, he'd invite the lonely old thing over.

The ladder was heavy for him also, but the two of them managed to get it positioned. They were a team.

"Thanks," she said. "I can just go on up."

What would it be like, being with someone like her, someone who could take care of herself? What would it be like, working together? He wondered, but he also insisted. If nothing else, he was a gentleman. "You stay here. Let me go up."

✳

After saying no, I'll do it over and over, even holding onto the ladder, trying to position herself so he could not start climbing, Cecilia realized she would have to push him away, would have to wrestle him for the ladder. "Okay. But just go in and unlock the door," she said. How would she explain the door being bolted from the inside? And what if Jay woke up? If Jay had locked the balcony door after all, she would be spared some embarrassment, but then Jay would win. The fire within her still smoldered. Even having this nice man know she and Jay were troubled was worth it if she won.

The shy cripple was watching through her sliding glass door now. Perhaps she was retarded. And the man—Carl, she thought his name was—was being watched by his wife, who stood outside, wearing what must be his jacket. Well, there was a bitch. The way she had pouted, looked angry at nothing the evening they were down. Poor Carl had nearly broken out in a sweat trying to make her smile. Cecilia knew it was hopeless, had imagined herself giving Carl the news flash. "She won't smile to save her life. To save your life." Still, she envied them. They were old and so had made it; their marriage had outlasted their looks, and she often wondered when she saw them on the parking lot, saw him open her door, hold her hand as they walked to the car, what he saw when he looked at her. Did he see the wrinkled, pinched face, the dyed hair, the loose skin that must cover her stomach, or did he see a young blond girl with blue eyes?

"I've been looking after my pigeons," she said before Carl started his climb. She remembered he had been interested in them. She would postpone the inevitable.

"The New Guinea ones?"

"Yes." Imagine him remembering that.

"Both parents care for the young," he said. "It's always impressed me."

"Both parents produce milk," she said.

"I suppose most of the care involves feeding. Only feeding. An animal to be envied." He started climbing, even though she tried one last time to talk him out of it.

"I love heights," she said. "You'll be taking away all my fun."

"Let him do it," the bitch said. "He needs to show off."

"It's a rickety ladder," Carl called from halfway up.

"You better hold it," the bitch said to Cecilia.

Cecilia did as she was told, wondering how something so heavy could also be rickety. She knew he would see her lie, knew she would be a topic of conversation afterwards. "Well," Carl would say in an urbane I've-seen-it-all way, "apparently the flaky girl had a fight with her husband. He'd locked her out. You know the kind of girl I mean, no judgment, silly, not enough sense to keep away from jerks. And the husband drinks. Just like a country western tearjerker. Poor kids." He'd laugh and shake his superior head. Just thinking about it made her hate Jay more than ever.

✳

The third rung from the top snapped in two when Carl stepped on it, and he tried to jump to the balcony, hold on with his arms and pull himself up. His body, though, was not as quick as his mind, and he did not grab the balcony railing fast enough. Instead and for no good reason, he kicked his left foot out, getting it caught in the wrought iron railing and knocking the ladder backwards. The ladder came down with a thud, barely missing Cecilia. Carl was hanging upside down by his left foot, and shouting, "Help me. Help. My foot's about to work loose."

Kate helped Cecilia with the ladder. Not so much helped as condescended to move, Cecilia thought as she watched Kate mince her way across the lawn. "I'm no good at this," Kate said before taking hold of a side of the ladder. What a surprise, Cecilia thought. When the ladder fell backwards a second time, Cecilia shouted, "Lean the same way I'm leaning. For God's sake." But it was no use. The bitch's incompetence, Cecilia decided, was too consistent to be accidental. "Think about your husband," Cecilia said as the ladder fell back on them again, and a fourth splinter pierced Cecilia's hand, this one up under a thumbnail.

"I'm trying. I'm just so weak. I can't do anything." Kate started to cry. "I've never been able to do anything."

"Help me," Carl called. "Hurry."

"See?" Kate said, giving up, sitting on the cold grass and drawing herself up into her husband's jacket. "He hates me. He knows I'm worthless."

It was a good scene, June thought, as Carl's cries hung in the February night and sounded hopeful, as if help were possible. A call implied a belief in a response, after all. She could build at least four plots with the three of them and the ladder, and that was not counting the snot-nosed husband June was sure was asleep upstairs. Wasn't that his Camaro in the lot? So with enough story material, she motored to the phone and dialed 911, told them to bring a ladder truck.

Kate had suspected that the girl was a fool, and now she was proving it, giving directions for the ladder as if she were an expert. If she knew so much, why had she asked for Carl's help? But Carl, hanging upside down, trying not to wave his arms, hoping his foot would hold, he was perfect. Forget the nude drawing. This was how she'd do him. Afraid to move. On the verge. Somewhere between redemption and a broken neck. Still pretending she was normal, pretending he could call to her in his need and she would respond. And that girl, hovering below him in a position to catch him if he fell, was as bad. Even she must see that was silly because if he did fall, he'd knock her to the ground as well. Yes, he was at his best now, hanging like that, his usual hopeless but still-trying self. And he probably would not break his neck, not really. He would just get a knock on the head, maybe sprain a wrist at the end of the arm he would try to catch himself with. He would deny he had expected worse, too, would say of course he had not expected a broken neck, but she could tell by his cries he was expecting one. Her art teacher would be impressed by the scene. Maybe he, at least, would know that she could do something after all. She stood and turned to go in for her drawing pad when the fire truck and the ambulance arrived. Both came with their sirens on high, their lights blazing. She would put them in the background.

✳

One fireman went up his own ladder, grabbed Carl around the waist, pulled his foot loose, and carried him down. It took minutes. Cecilia wanted to rush up the ladder while it was still in place, but another fireman stopped her. "Please," she said. "I'm locked out. I just want to get up to my balcony door. That's how this all happened." The fireman shook his head. He seemed to have no response but disgust. "Please, please, please," she said. "I'll pay you."

✳

"The virgin and the firefighter," June wrote across the top of her yellow legal pad. Who would have thought her own apartment building could supply so many plots? She may have to stay up all night.

✳

"I'm fine," Carl said from his position on the stretcher as the paramedics checked him. The idiots would not let him up until they finished their ritual. As if he did not feel enough like a weakling, a useless old man. Kate was standing over him, beaming, her eyes sparkling. He turned away and pushed the stethoscope away in one movement. "Let me up." He shouted it, and they did. If it were up to Kate, he would have hung there all night, would have had to either sleep like a bat or fall head first. "And for God's sake, help the girl get into her apartment."

The firefighter who had carried him down climbed up to the balcony and slid open the glass door. "Just open the front door," Cecilia said. "I'll meet you there." She ran up the inside stairs, relieved that it would only be the fireman who would know of her rotten marriage.

Jay was being attacked from all sides by creatures he could not see clearly. He could hear their snarls, though, feel their hot breath on his back, their sharp teeth gnawing at his heels. Alongside him, keeping pace, was a wagon of some kind, larger than a chariot. It was burning, and he saw it was swerving, starting to turn into him. There was nothing to do but prepare for the pain. The pain had to come. Yet still he ran faster, ran from the pain that would come. As fast as his weak legs would carry him. Faster and faster.

Just as the fireman stepped into the living room, he heard a thump, then a yelp. As he turned toward the sound—toward the direction of the sound—expecting a puppy, a large puppy, a naked young man ran at him. "Run," the man shouted. "As fast as you can."

"Hold on, now," the fireman said. "I'm only here to help."

Jay screamed and swung, and the fireman ducked, then grabbed Jay's arm and turned him around, held him from behind. When Jay awoke he was in his living room, and he was being held from behind by a strange man. "Take it easy," the man holding him said. He heard Cecilia calling from outside the door. "Let me in. Just let me in."

"You weren't going to help me," Carl said to Kate. They were waiting outside for something else to happen, for the fireman to come back down, for the episode to end. They had heard Jay's scream.

"I knew he was home all the time," Kate said.

"You are selfish," Carl said. "More selfish than I ever realized."

"She should leave him," Kate said. "Why stay with someone like that?"

"She won't leave," Carl said, knowing it was true as he said it. She believed in forever, in putting up with it all, in pretending. He knew her type. In sickness and in health, even if health meant just a little less sick.

Cecilia closed the door on the fireman, looked at Jay, still naked and starting to shiver a little. I got in, she would say. I won. "Let's go to bed," she said, taking him by the hand. "We can talk about this tomorrow." He stumbled, fell against her, and she hugged him. He grinned at her diagonally. His eyes were watery, blank. He was not entirely awake. Of course, he also had had a rough night, probably no dinner, probably twelve beers, each twenty minutes or less, and those horrid nightmares that continually plagued him. Honey, she thought as she led him down the hall. His skin was cold. You darling boy. "Poor Baby."

June was parked once again by her computer. She was not tired anyway, and if she could just get one more out tonight, or rather this morning, she would recover the cost of her chair that much faster. She had in mind a story about a young girl and an older man doing terrible things to the young girl's husband, things that made the young man scream. One of her better-paying magazines preferred the slightly sadistic twist.

Kate and Carl watched the fire truck and the ambulance pull away, turn down Iron Street and disappear into the darkness. "What else am I?" she asked. She stood close, looked up at his darkened face.

"Besides selfish?"

"Besides selfish."

"Mean," he said. "You're mean."

"I knew it," she said. "I always knew it."

✶

And upstairs in Apartment D, as Sheila Baker slept a deep drug-induced sleep, she reached for the bulk and warmth of Joe, her hand moving restlessly over the cool sheet, trying to prove to her body what the drugs had already convinced her brain: all was as it should be. It was possible to go on.

KING HEROD DIED OF CANCER

At first, there were stories about Father Fisher that had the feel of jokes. "Did you hear what he said about King Herod at midnight mass?" "Have you heard him sing all six verses of 'Mary, Our Mother'?" "Did you hear he told the religion class at St. Elizabeth's Academy that only ugly girls danced with one another?" "And what about poor Joe Baker's funeral, about standing right there in front of the casket and saying that the produce Joe sold and passed off as fresh was not, that Joe had operated his business on the sucker principle?" Usually the parishioners of Holy Cross laughed, reducing Father Fisher and anything he could say to the level of a Vice President of the United States or a senile ancestor. Some, of course, did not see the humor. Some few claimed to be distracted by the off-key but relentless singing, by the use of the pulpit to say whatever irreverent or screwball thing came into his head. He interfered with their piety, they told Father Mullamphy, the pastor. Something had to be done.

Father Mullamphy, his young, untroubled face tanned from his twice-weekly golf outings, nodded, tsk-tsk'd, and agreed one hundred percent, but made no promises. That was the strategy, the approach to conflict his few detractors often cited, that had made him the youngest pastor in the St. Louis Archdiocese. Father Mullamphy himself told Father Fisher jokes to the five other priests from his seminary class that he played poker with every Thursday evening, but explained that Father Fisher needed a place to work, a home. Without those, he would be back on the psychiatric ward taking tranquilizers as if they were breath mints and conversing with the Holy Spirit. Also, and Father Mullamphy admitted it freely, someone had to take the early masses and hear the confessions scheduled for every other Saturday.

Father Fisher was good at confession. He considered it his specialty, and that in itself was another oddity. Confession in a dark booth, sins whispered through a screen, or any kind of confession for that matter, was out of style. It had gone out in the early sixties with the Latin mass and head coverings for women. But just as some grandmothers and great-grandmothers still said the rosary every night, there were some parishioners who wanted to confess often and who preferred the secrecy of the confessional. Father Fisher preferred the anonymous method, too. He liked the challenge of guessing the sinner's identity, calling him by name at the end for shock value, perhaps asking after the wife and kids.

There were those, too, whom he refused to forgive. He would not grant absolution for lukewarm, insipid sins that started as good intentions. Natalie Ross, a pretty and sincere St. Elizabeth's girl, was one he refused. In trying to fix a shy classmate up with a prom date, Natalie had humiliated and embarrassed the girl, had made her feel even more unwanted. And what Natalie had done was not even a sin, not technically anyway, but though Father Fisher explained that, Natalie showed up every other Saturday and through the screen that glistened gold in the half light asked God to forgive her.

"I cannot do it," Father Fisher said, each time.

"Come on, Father," Natalie would answer. "I'm asking God, not you."

"Then go through someone else. Through me, He says no."

And after a time, Father Fisher began teasing Natalie if he saw her as he chaperoned a teen dance or greeted worshippers after Sunday mass. "See you Saturday," he would say and wink to make her blush to the brown roots of her blond hair. She reminded him of girls he used to date before he entered the seminary, girls who wore dotted swiss dresses and crinoline petticoats and who giggled when he asked them out. She reminded him, too, of the therapists and social workers and aides he had tried in vain to avoid while in the hospital. He suspected she came to him every other Saturday to help him as much as herself, to make him feel useful. He was sure of it. She was a well-meaning bitch who had caught the scent of a wounded soul.

Another of Father Fisher's penitents was Jerry Schneider, a hardware salesman in his mid-forties who cheated on his wife, the beautiful Sally Schneider so admired in the parish for her generosity and high spirits, cheated on her with ugly women with dyed black hair and hand-drawn eyebrows, sullen women with varicose veins, or barrel-chested den-mother types who perspired freely. Father forgave Jerry every time, because adultery was a real sin. No matter how poor his choices, Jerry was not trying to help anyone but himself.

Real sins deserved real forgiveness. That had been his message at the midnight mass people laughed about. "King Herod," he had said, "killed babies. Herod and his men killed babies without any thought but themselves. They weren't trying to help the babies, but—'oh my'—killed them accidentally. They were evil. And evil was and is necessary." Once he had become convinced that evil was indeed important, once he had decided his mother's misery had come from her own decisions and not from evil, and so there would be no corresponding good, he wanted to tell everyone. People should see the paradox. He preached against and condemned evil yet knew it would not disappear, and knew it must not. "Where would Christ be," he had said at that midnight mass, "without evil? If Herod had been a litterer instead of a baby killer, if Herod had been confused, nutritionally deficient, who would need a savior? Would Jesus Christ have sweat blood and died because people talked in theaters or masturbated?"

Naturally that last word was the one some parishioners complained about or laughed at. The eighth-grade boys seemed to find it especially funny, and while one or two of them had always been able to get a laugh by doing Father Fisher, the whole group tried to do him now. Some could actually look like Father Fisher by combing their brown hair into bangs, stuffing a backpack under their jackets, and looking at their feet as they walked. They would take big steps and mutter as he did, "little shits, little mittenless shits." And they added masturbating now. "Mittenless

masturbating shits." Sometimes they sang "Mary, Our Mother" to
the tune of "Camptown Races" as Father Fisher had done once at
the children's mass. They added the doo-dah's, too, which he had
not. Father Fisher was aware of but unaffected by the mimicry. It
was not true evil, but at least it was not well-intentioned.

When the parish's May Spring Fling came around again, the
committee members voted to keep Father Fisher uninvolved.
They remembered the previous year, his first year in the parish,
when he had acted without authority and hired an accordion
player, one, it was rumored, who was a former fellow inmate. The
committee chairperson this year, however, was Beatrice Cooney,
Father Mullamphy's cousin, who cooked for the two priests on
Monday and Tuesday evenings. Not many priests had house-
keepers anymore—at about the time mandatory head coverings
for women were done away with, the idea that a priest could not
cook or clean for himself had appeared absurd—but most had a
relative or some good-hearted parishioner who helped out now
and then. Beatrice was the helper at Holy Cross, and she was both
a parishioner and a relative. She was also, Father Fisher knew, a
do-gooder busybody and a rotten cook to boot. She made three
things: taco salad, tuna casserole, and lasagna. Of the three, her
lasagna was the crunchiest. Father Mullamphy courteously ate
her meals, cleaning his plate but never asking for seconds. Father
Fisher simply pushed his plate aside, untouched, and ordered a
pizza later.

But as Beatrice told her bingo group, she did not think much of
Father Fisher, either. In fact, she was one of the primary sources of
Father Fisher jokes. She was the one who told how he would lean
back in his chair right in the middle of a dinner he would not eat,
even if no one had spoken for five or ten minutes, and say "Horse
piss!" just out of the blue like that. And one time he passed her
the sugar for her iced tea before he took any and said, "Age before
beauty," even though everyone knew he was at least three years
older than she, and no one but kids said stuff like that. And he
stirred his tea for such a long time, too. The clink, clink, clink of the
spoon against the glass almost drove her and Bobby (what, as a
cousin, she was entitled to call Father Mullamphy) to distraction.

And as he stirred his iced tea, Father Fisher often thought about cause and effect and meaning in chaos and why the whirlpool was so easily started. It was as if the slightest motion could cause all liquid, maybe all things, spinning meaninglessly downward. He also wondered how long he could stir his tea and stare thoughtfully into his glass before Beatrice would ask him to stop, which she never did.

As the committee chairperson, in spite of her determination to keep all plans from Father Fisher, Beatrice could not help letting a few things slip. Maybe, Father Fisher thought, all his stirring weakened her resolve. She said that ticket sales were slower than usual, and that the committee members were providing the hot hors d'oeuvres to save money on catering. Beatrice herself was making cocktail weenies in a sweet-n-sour sauce. "I mean for a couple's ticket, fifteen dollars, you get the River City Rats and snacks, good ones, too. The drinks, of course, are extra. I do not understand it," she said. "The River City Rats do 'Heartbreak Hotel' so well, I just close my eyes and sway." She shrugged her narrow shoulders and shook her small cantaloupe-shaped head. "Well, people are just too busy now."

Father Fisher, though, had another explanation. He said the River City Rats played the kind of AM radio music that was meant as a break from the commercials. The fact that he had never heard of, much less heard, the River City Rats did not daunt him in his attack. The whole point of music like that was to sell Fords or sleeper sofas. He said, too, that nothing sounded less appetizing than hot dogs mired in heavy syrup, and he considered it a tribute to the intelligence level of the parish that tickets were hard to sell. "In fact," he said, "it would surprise me if you could give them away."

He continued in that vein for a while, adding that no one could pay him enough to show up—to which Beatrice said, "Thank God," under her breath—until he got to the part about the committee having its head up its collective ass, and Beatrice screamed. "See how he talks," she said to Father Mullamphy, her blue eyes glowing, a bony finger pointing at Father Fisher. "Can't you control him, Bobby? Isn't he supposed to take pills or something?"

Of course, Father Fisher had every intention of not only going to the dance as part of his parish duty, but also trying to swell the crowd. When Jerry Schneider came for confession a week before the dance and told about taking Sally's manicurist to an East St. Louis disco and motel, Father Fisher forgave him, but gave a stiffer penance than the usual Our Fathers and Hail Marys. He told Jerry to buy a couple's ticket and bring Sally to the May Spring Fling.

"Sure, Father," Jerry said. "And one more thing. I think Sally has someone else."

"Oh?" Father Fisher could say no more, for he had lately become Sally's confessor and knew Jerry was right.

"Can you forgive me for wanting to kill her?"

"No question about it. I once wanted to kill a social worker nun who kept telling me I was making the world better, something that is both impossible and undesirable, by the way, by doing the Lord's work. I'd try to upset her by saying, 'What's He doing then?' or 'If I'm doing His, who's doing mine?' But that just encouraged her, made her work harder on my case. Eventually I did nothing but pray for her demise."

"I knew I could count on you, Father," Jerry said. "You're nuts."

Father Fisher had forgiven Sally's adultery, too, just as he always did Jerry's. They were the easy ones, sinners of big sins. He continued to resist Natalie, though, even when she said, "I hear you're granting absolution for the price of a dance ticket."

"Jerry has a big mouth," he said, and wondered at his penitents discussing him. It seemed a violation of something, some church rule, or at least a particular interpretation of a church rule.

But Natalie did not want it Jerry's way. She had what she called a "more noble" idea. She would buy an eight-dollar stag ticket and give it to Amelia Federman with an offer to babysit. Amelia was a young widow with a six-year-old son who had cerebral palsy. She was the sentimental favorite of the parish, and a natural target for Natalie's do-gooder impulses.

"That won't get you absolution," Father Fisher said, and without warning was overcome with disgust at himself for wasting his time among the well-meaning, the charitable, the soft and soggy.

There were not as many clear-cut cases of evil as there should be. Most sins lately could be reduced to no-fault nothingness. His mother had suffered most of her life, but there had been no one responsible. Her boss at the all-night bakery could have paid her more, but she had turned down two jobs her son knew of, saying she liked the bakery job. Well, her husband should not have died so early, not before his son was born, but that was no one's fault, either. And the fire that did not destroy but ruined the house, that left the whole thing so charred it could not be cleaned but had to be lived with until they could afford to paint it, had been caused by friendly neighbors wanting to help his poor mother by cooking breakfast, helpers so eager one of them forgot to turn off the broiler.

"Listen," he said to Natalie through the screen, said to the girl who he knew knelt straight and quiet as if picturing herself not only good but misunderstood and therefore better for bearing the heavy cross of crazy Father Fisher, who wanted to help him in order to confirm her own opinion of herself as saintly. A good girl. "Don't come back. Get absolution from Father Mullamphy. Become a Lutheran. You nauseate me."

A week later when he saw Amelia Federman swish into the church basement in a backless purple chiffon dress, looking like a pretty woman instead of a widow with an afflicted son, he thought perhaps Natalie's meddling had helped. He smiled at Amelia from his self-appointed post at the ticket table, and even smiled a few times at the bony Beatrice who wore what looked like an orange sack, and who really did close her eyes when the River City Rats struck their first chord. And Beatrice, who had told her bingo group he was talking to the Holy Spirit again, not praying either, just complaining, saying, "Where is all this wisdom you promised?" and so (mark her words) would be leaving soon, smiled back. By the time the Schneiders arrived, Sally was just another pretty woman in a full-skirted dress, one more flower in the bouquet. Beauties all. But though Father Fisher smiled at Sally as at all the others, she appeared not to see him; it was as if her eyes would not focus. Well, that was the way with some sinners. Even after being forgiven, they would act as if the whole thing were the confessor's fault.

After the ice was broken by the courageous few who did not mind being stared at, the dance floor became crowded. Things had changed a lot since a young Harry Fisher took girls like Natalie to dances. There always had been a few girls, usually the fat and fancy as he had said at St. Elizabeth's, who danced together, who seemed confident no males would ask, and who acted as if they did not care. But now, many women danced with one another and let the poor men catch up, join in if they could. Three of the prettiest went out for one number, and gyrated, swayed, and glided all over the dance floor, seemingly not even aware of one another, let alone the men who joined in late and tried to be their partners. Oh sure, there were the traditional man and woman couples, too, but Father Fisher once counted eleven stray females on the floor. The beautiful Sally Schneider, a bouncy and vigorous dancer, was usually one of these, even though Jerry had tried to dance with her more than once.

Father Fisher watched from his self-appointed welcoming post, shifting his weight from one foot to the other, talking about nothing to those arriving. The parishioners said it was a nice night, a good crowd, a good band. They said the weather was going to be pleasant for a few days, the peonies were in full bloom, and an event like this made them wish they could dance. No one asked about evil, about the need for it, about the fact that too much could be explained away by motives. He knew they would have considered such talk out of place at a dance. He knew many things he said were considered out of place, were not understood.

He had told the girls at St. Elizabeth's that the Blessed Virgin Mary—the BVM as he called her—never cut her hair, and to be like her, they should never cut theirs. When one of the young teachers complained, a cute, earnest, short-haired teacher, clearly trained in educational theory, he tried to explain that it had been a joke. For God's sake, didn't she know a joke when she heard one? How could anyone know something like that about the BVM? Why would anyone care? Well that, she said, was her point exactly.

So as he stood at the ticket table and watched the dance, really just a swirl of spring pastels if he crossed his eyes, he told himself what he had been telling himself for years, what the rectors at the seminary had hinted at long ago. His loneliness was chronic. His best conversations were destined to be with himself. He may as well go up to his room.

And as Father Fisher was getting ready to leave, though still standing and smiling by the entrance, Jerry Schneider walked slowly from the folding-table-bar on one side of the dance floor, all the way across to the other side to Sally, dancing with herself and with three other women, Amelia Federman included. Sally's back was to him, and he grabbed her shoulder with his left hand, then swung hard and fast with his right when she turned. Sally jerked her head back, though, and his fist missed her chin. The force of what would have been a powerful punch pulled him off balance and he stumbled heavily into Amelia, pushing her backwards about five feet until she fell, finally, on her back on top of a cart of unfolded metal folding chairs. Jerry fell on top of her.

Amelia screamed. Jerry jumped up and screamed, too. "I'm sorry. Oh, God. I'm sorry." Many of the parishioners screamed as well, screamed for an ambulance, cursed at Jerry, cried out along with Amelia as if they could feel her pain. The River City Rats continued to play "Proud Mary."

"I was aiming at my wife," Jerry said to the crowd. "I really was."

✳

By eight o'clock mass the following Thursday morning, the parishioners knew three discs in Amelia's back had been crushed and that the scheduled surgery could be just the first of many. So Father Fisher decided to talk again about evil, even though the nine gray-headed women and the two men, one permanently bent so that in his natural state he watched his shoes, had not asked for insights or wisdom, and would, he knew, be annoyed at a homily of any kind at what was meant to be a fast mass.

"King Herod was a baby killer. And a good one. Like Jerry Schneider, he did not have anything against those he hurt. They were in his way. He was evil. He was greedy and jealous and mean. Jerry Schneider slaughters the innocent." He paused to look at the crowd. He did not want them to start daydreaming before he got to his point, whatever that would be. "My mother was a victim of nothing except namby-pamby do-gooders who deserve to be spat out of the mouth of God for being flavorless, lukewarm mush. Natalie Ross is one." He wanted to talk about Jerry, though. Not Natalie. "She, too, helped in the slaughter of the innocent. But Jerry. Jerry. King Jerry Schneider the baby killer is evil like we have not had among us for a long time. Evil like we need!" He shouted so even those hard of hearing would catch on. "I am the one who time and time again told Jerry God forgave him. I am the one." He hit his breast twice. "It was I. And I was right. God forgave. He forgives. He forgives the sinners because He needs the evil ones. The adulterers, fornicators, and baby killers."

Father Mullamphy stood at the far entrance to the sacristy and motioned for him. Beatrice was behind Father Mullamphy on the phone. Father Fisher saw this and decided to hurry. "The girls at St. Elizabeth's have no sense of humor. It is something I have to say. My time is running out. Joe Baker sold rotten produce. I don't know what else he did. He never confessed. And another thing. Natalie Ross and Bob Mullamphy are purveyors of Christian Charity. Beatrice Cooney is a busybody. My mother's neighbors were helpful. None of them can be forgiven. Ever. Each is a little spider mite, a speck of dust, a piece of junk mail."

Father Mullamphy walked toward the pulpit, pausing to genuflect before the altar. He was robed to say mass, to take over.

"Jerry has had many women. His wife is an adulterer, too. They are big sinners. Worth dying for. Could Christ have died for Bob here? For Bob Mullamphy and his doo-dah charity?"

Father Mullamphy took him from behind, grabbed him at each elbow and walked him backwards from the pulpit to the closed sacristy door. "You will never eradicate evil. God needs it," Father Fisher said, still shouting so he could be heard even away from the microphone. He moved back easily as Father Mullamphy guided him, but continued to explain. The people should know the whole ugly truth. "King Herod died of cancer." He did not know what that meant. The pressure on his elbows made concentrating difficult. He had lost track, but he knew he was right. "Ask yourselves what that means."

I Want Myron

B ridget Donnelly wanted Myron MacDonald for an evening or two of fun, nothing more serious. She said that
to herself as she sat at her small, round table in the Red
Rooster Sports Bar and watched him carry a tray of combination
dinners to a noisy threesome. His running shorts were royal blue
and silky, and the hair on the back of his legs grew sparser and
darker as it neared the shorts. Nothing more serious than fun,
she said, and noticed he moved through the tables like a beagle
through the woods—no grace or style, but an adorable quickness
and energy, a happy backside.

He was her waiter, and he was twenty years younger, and his
name meant pleasure, and he was a man of big ideas. He liked
older women and people who tipped well and musicians of all
kinds though he could not carry a tune. He had told her all of this
and more over the previous two evenings as she sat at the same
table she sat at now, letting him know she had stopped in for the
fried clams originally but had come back for him.

She told him she drove a refuse truck for the city of St. Louis and
told him (too late) not to laugh because it was a good, well-paying
job, a better one than a sociology major had a right to expect. Last
night, she told him her name meant strength, but did not tell
him Myron meant pleasant, not pleasure—she had looked it up.
She told him on the first night that two micks like them would
be doubly bad together so he would think of them together, and
she told him of her grandfather's two mick classifications: lace
curtain and carey patch. The lace curtain Irish would gladly give

75

you the shirt off someone else's back, and the carey patch Irish would take the shirt and sell it for drink.

Tonight she told him it was her forty-fifth birthday, an outright lie. These were the nights of enervating stillness typical of a Midwest August, and her birthday was in March, but she wanted to provide a reason for celebration, a cause for drawing closer. In fact, she had passed forty-five six years earlier, had passed it going so fast the whole year was a blur. Forty-five was the year she had been engaged to Stephen, a bank clerk and a sculptor who had talked her into having her stomach muscles cut and then tucked, having her eyeliner tattooed on. Stephen was just one memento of a derailed life, her flat stomach and accented eyes souvenirs of nothing. She wished it were otherwise and wanted to believe the words of Leon, the civil engineer she had had before Stephen. "Nothing is truly nothing," he said. "Everything is something."

Even without the eyeliner and the tummy tuck, Bridget would have been attractive. She had thick hair that fell to her shoulders, heavy with shine, the few gray strands at her temples visible only when she pushed the dark mass back, held it there with a headband as she did tonight. Her face was round and dimpled, her eyes dark and wide set, their lids slightly droopy. Her lips were cushiony, surrounded by only a few pucker lines as delicate as ice crystals on window glass. It was those lines that betrayed her age, as well as the loose skin at the base of her neck and the occasional facial puffiness that after an especially entertaining night could stay all during her route.

"When I was a teenager," Myron said as he sat at her table, his customers giving him a short break, "I wanted to be two things. Rich and sexy. I soon learned that everyone, almost everyone, can be sexy, but I still want to be rich."

She nodded and watched him tilt his heavy glass mug back as he finished his beer, and the mug absorbed some of the already dim bar light. She had never wanted to be rich, but she agreed that anyone could be desirable to someone else, to many someone elses. Her men stretched back thirty-seven years to her fourteenth year when she started going steady with Ed Nesbitt, whose father was an official in the meat cutters' union and so supplied the bratwurst for his son's high school's fall festival fund raisers. Ed was the beginning of the line, Bridget always thought, discounting the grade school loves and crushes who only blushed and giggled. Ed actually picked her up on his bicycle, let her ride the handlebars on their trip to the abandoned record center's parking lot where he kissed her and gave her his mother's old friendship ring.

Lately Bridget pictured her men in a conga line, kicking and hopping in time (and some sadly rhythmless ones out of time), waving to her as they bounced past, making her make promises she knew would not be kept, asking her with their eyes for a dance, a kiss, a future. You are lots of fun, Bridget Donnelly, they said. Never the wet blanket. Why are we here, she asked each member of the dance troupe as he wiggled and bounced by. What's the point? Will we be remembered? Missed? They winked, nodded, blew her kisses. She was asking the sloppy weepy drunk questions, and they all knew there was no need to answer. But she was not drunk, not even in her fantasy. She was too old. Her cast iron stomach was long gone, her recovery time too slow.

"I could be rich by the time I'm forty," Myron said. He kicked the table as he crossed his legs, sloshing beer from her still-full mug onto the scarred wood of the table top.

"Sure you could be. Anyone could be," she said. "Except me, of course."

"You'll be rich by the time you're fifty," he said.

She smiled.

"Besides," he said. "I'll share. I'll buy you whatever you want."

"A house on a beach. Call it a late birthday present."

"You got it," he said as someone at a far table waved him over. Two of his tables wanted more drinks and dessert, and his just-cleared deuce filled up again. Bridget ordered a patty melt once when he passed, and when he delivered it, he was close to breathless. "Hell," he said. "I shouldn't work so hard on your birthday. How about if we get that beach house soon. What about Tahiti?"

She sipped her warm and flat beer and then smiled at him. "I think I could stand it."

"Shit," he said as the threesome's five other friends arrived and they all started pushing tables together. "Gotta go. Keep thinking of Tahiti."

But she pictured the conga line instead. She had enjoyed all her men, had wanted them first with her body, her molecules singing out to theirs, wanting a bond, and her mind agreeing, approving, responding. And she had not used and discarded her men, had never intended for any of her liaisons to end, had at least admitted the possibility of some future with each one. Well, more or less. She would concede Myron and a few like him were temporary from the first molecular note, but most had been what her mother called *keepers*. But they had all finally been *too* something: too clinging, too bossy, too loud, too drunk, too lazy, too confused, too silly, too dull, or too busy. She had been engaged to four of them, but none were right for the long haul. Now at fifty-one, she knew the haul was considerably shorter. Her mother called her unusually picky, said most married women took one of the *too*'s and made do.

Her father had said the same this past February after she had gone to Joe Baker's funeral with her parents. Though a bit younger than her parents, closer to her age in fact, Joe had been their good friend, and his death, combined with the beers her father downed at the funeral party, had caused her father to come right out with it. He had called it a frank discussion, taking the bull by the horns. "No use beating around the bush any longer. You should not have broken all those engagements," he said, holding her by the shoulders to make his point clear in the widow's apartment near the end of the funeral party. "I don't care what the hell you do for a job or career or whatever you want to call it, but a woman like you, one who is still sort of good looking, should have reproduced."

"I'm like the Bakers," she had answered. "I'm a renter, not a buyer."

"I've decided something," Myron said now as he sat again next to her. "I've decided you should get rip-roaring drunk on your forty-fifth." He pushed an Old Fitzgerald on the rocks he carried, and she had assumed was his, over to her. "Me, too." He took the drink back and took a sip. "You'd do the same for me if I were forty-five."

When it was her turn to sip, she placed her mouth exactly where his had been. "When will that be?"

"What be?"

"When you're forty-five."

"Fourteen years from now. Well, not now. Fourteen years and a few months."

"We'll meet here for it. Same place, same time, fourteen years and some months from now."

"This dump?" he said. "We'll be in Tahiti. Don't try to get out of it, now. You promised." He took the whiskey back and killed it.

"Waiter," someone called from the large group in the back.

"I think that's you," she said.

"Me? God, what a life. Can I ride in your garbage truck some time?"

At least twice a week lately, Bridget totaled up her fifty-one and a half years, made a list of good and bad, then looked at it before sliding in between her sheets. The big orange tank, number 463–10 with its new shocks, was invariably in the good column, one of the few items that ended up in the good column no matter what her mood. She enjoyed the idea of herself, Bridget Donnelly, a woman who could squeeze into a pair of size seven jeans as she had done for tonight, maneuvering a monstrous, noisy machine through streets and alleys. She liked the B. *Donnelly* stenciled in two-inch letters on the door, just below where she hung her elbow.

In the bad column were eleven previous jobs, all boring or low paying or demeaning or phony, jobs like direct mail marketing, like telephone sales, like assistant administrator of Elderly Entertainment Incorporated (which meant arranging for a group of teenagers to belt out spirituals off-key to captives in nursing homes). She had wasted so much of her life, the prime of it, she wrote down but hoped not, in a desultory search for something she would like to do, could do, would be allowed to do. Not until she was forty-eight did she date a man whose friend was in charge of refuse department hiring and so stumble into trash hauling, as she guessed all the trash haulers had. No one ever said, "I want to be a garbage man or woman when I grow up." And she was not the only woman, either. That battle had been fought by someone feistier than she ten or fifteen years earlier.

Her chronic indigestion was also in the bad column, as were the kerosene smell from the metal plating plants on the river a mile away from her apartment, the new people in her neighborhood who called their children mother-fucker, her extra heavy periods, her stiffening joints, her new allergy to chocolate, and her parents' frowning faces. They wished they could brag about her at the senior center cocktail parties, wished she had at least one child so they could die knowing their genes would be carried on. The most important reason for living, her father said often as her mother nodded in the background, was self-perpetuation. All else was vanity, what he called "playing some made-up game without rules."

The night of Joe Baker's funeral, he had explained. "Life is over in a flash. And for what? It must be *for* something, see? I mean that's what I think. You have to leave something behind." He was almost crying, and she knew that leaving her behind was not the meaning he had hoped for for himself; she was not enough to leave.

"So," Myron said as he sat once more at her table. "When are we going to Maui?" He polished off her beer.

"Tahiti," she said. "You said Tahiti."

"Okay. We'll go there. What's the difference? Whatever it is, I'll probably never notice."

"You don't want me with you in Tahiti. You'll pick up a brown-skinned dancing girl, the kind who does the fast swivel hula."

"I want you," Myron said and placed both hands over his heart. "My garbage lassie, my colleen of the landfill."

It was an hour until closing time, so when Myron's customers beckoned him again, Bridget went to the bar for a cup of coffee. She kept it at the table for him, on his next visit told him to drink it. "Great idea," he said. "Caffeine, the fuel of champions." He slurped it, then moved behind the bar and drew himself another mug.

In the last fifteen minutes of the Red Rooster's business day, after Myron took all the last-call orders, he gave Bridget a back rub. There were only four other customers by that time anyway, and only three were awake. He was not much in demand, he told her, as he slipped his hands under her T-shirt and rubbed the muscles covering her spine, worked them until they felt like silken pads, like down, like spun sugar. He told her he was a trained masseur. He had stopped short of getting his license, though he could not remember why. She nodded, her neck like a strand of cotton.

They were singing "k k k Katie, k k k Katie" when they were pulled over. "I'll be waiting at your k k k kitchen door," Bridget sang as Myron eased his old Buick onto the shoulder of Highway 40 near the zoo. Myron said, "Top o' the morning, Officer," and the officer said, "License." He was a black man about Bridget's age with red rimmed eyes.

"You were all over the road," the officer said. "Only half in any lane. You were doing eighty-five."

"Sorry," Myron said, then turned to Bridget and smiled. "As you can see, I was distracted by this beautiful colleen."

"Step out of the car," the officer said. "Step out slowly. Bring your keys." He shone his flashlight around inside the Buick, illuminated a few shiny gum wrappers on the back seat, a crumpled cash register receipt on the floor by Bridget's feet. When Myron stepped out, the policeman led him to the back, and Bridget turned to watch. The other policeman was out of the car by then, waiting at Myron's trunk. She heard their voices, distorted by the highway noises, the still and moist air of an early August morning. The other officer was young, white, and chubby.

She saw Myron shake his head, his voice angry. She got out of his car, leaned on it near the passenger's door to hear but not to disrupt or intrude.

They wanted him to open his trunk; they wanted to give him a breath test. No. He said he knew he did not have to take the test. No. Charge him with recklessness, take him in, get it over with, or leave him alone. They could not force him to breathe. They were pigs. He would do nothing for them, not even if they beat him senseless.

Of course, they did open his trunk; she wondered why they had asked. She stood at the side of the car, facing them, no longer leaning, visible enough so they would know she was a witness to a beating, to any violation of Myron's rights. But she could not see what was in the trunk, and their expressions showed little but general disgust.

They cuffed Myron and placed him in the back of the patrol car, pushing his head down so he would fit. The chubby one threw Myron's keys in her direction. "Can you drive?" He did not wait for an answer, but continued even as she bent to retrieve the keys from the littered shoulder. "Follow us to Station One, Sublette Avenue. Your boyfriend may need his car."

"I drive a refuse truck," she said, but he had already turned back, was squeezing himself into the first-district car. "So I guess I can drive anything," she said even as the police car eased out onto the highway. Luckily she knew where the Sublette station was.

✳

She entered the station through double glass doors that led to a foyer and another set of doors that opened into a large square room with white walls and a white tile floor. Two women sat on a long, high-backed bench in the middle of the far wall. A young policeman, no older then twenty-five, was behind a counter, so she asked him for Myron. "Talk to Wickes," he said.

"What?"

"Wickes. Sergeant Wickes."

"I want Myron MacDonald."

"She'll be here soon." The young policeman looked at a computer screen as he talked.

"I'm not looking for a she," Bridget said as Sergeant Wickes entered through a door behind the counter. She also was quite a few years younger than Bridget. She had an English choirboy face, and she kept her hat on. All incoming were processed downstairs, Wickes said, and no, Bridget could not go down there. She pointed to the hard bench, and said Bridget could wait there if she so chose. She would be called.

"How long?" Bridget asked, and Wickes shrugged, half smiled as if asking herself why she heard the same stupid question night after night. "Don't you want my name?" Bridget asked. "I mean, how else can you call me?" Wickes rolled her eyes, shook her head, then said Bridget could give her name if it would make her feel better. Bridget said it would take much more than that, but it was a start. "Bridget Donnelly," she said, and added "city employee," as if it would make a difference. She watched Wickes write it down.

She sat beside the two women and leaned her head against the wooden bench back and closed her eyes. It was 2 A.M. Her route started at six-thirty. She should just leave Myron's keys at the desk, take a cab back to the Red Rooster's parking lot, drive home, and sleep for about three hours. After all, Myron was no one to her. A mature, experienced woman had no business sitting in a depressing though brightly lit police super station waiting for a young and apparently foolish and probably drunk and maybe criminal man just because he had promised her fun and an even better massage.

"I'm tempted to leave him here this time," one of the two women said.

"Right," the other said. "Let 'im rot."

She opened her eyes and looked at the acoustic tiles above. If she left his keys, how likely was he to end up with them? If she left, there would be no one in the whole world who knew his plight, who waited for his release, who was on his side. He had seemed helpless in his anger. There was a small round table in the far corner of the overly chilled room, a table about the size of the one she had spent five hours at tonight. It was empty. The crime business seemed slow this Wednesday morning. The chubby policeman had said "boyfriend" as if it were a perversion, as if someone should make a law against it.

Wickes had been replaced at the desk by a matronly Asian woman wearing a brown cardigan over a lace-trimmed, white blouse. She sat at the opposite end of the counter from the young policeman and stared at another computer screen. "Where is Myron MacDonald now?" Bridget asked after approaching the counter. Neither answered. "Excuse me," she said.

"Yes?" The woman in the cardigan looked up.

"Where is Myron MacDonald now?"

"And who are you?"

"A friend. I have his car keys."

"And who is he?"

"A prisoner, I guess," she said. "Or a detainee. A possible prisoner, a suspected criminal? I don't know what to call him."

The woman looked at her computer screen. "Name?"

"Myron MacDonald."

"Capital D?"

"I would imagine."

"Middle initial?"

"I have no idea."

"Age?"

"Thirty-one."

"Date of birth?"

"Don't know."

"You don't know much about your friends," the woman said, triumph in her voice as if she had caught Bridget impersonating a friend, was on her way to uncovering a conspiracy.

Bridget blushed. She knew he wanted to go to Tahiti or Maui, knew he liked older women and big tippers. "His name means pleasant," she said.

"Well, he's still here. He's not been charged." The phone beside the young man in uniform began ringing, but he made no move to answer it.

"What happens next? When will he be charged?" Bridget watched the young policeman look at the ringing phone.

"Depends," the woman said, and moved down to the other end of the counter to answer the phone. Bridget stood and listened to a series of yeses, uh-huhs, rights, and sures. "I'll be in the rest room if you need me," she said to the woman, who gave no indication of having heard. The young policeman looked away when she glanced at him.

The rest room was as clean and bright and cold and sad as the waiting room. Bridget stood before the mirror under the fluorescent light. She looked as bad as she had expected, as bad as fifty-one years could look after three evenings in a row in a smoky bar with flat beers and fried foods. Beneath her eyes were two smooth and purple puffs, and the lines from her nose to the corners of her lips were dark and definite. "Crappy lighting," she said to her reflection. "We don't really look this bad." She rubbed her palms over her breasts, warming them. Fate had elected her Myron's advocate; pop-up nipples would not help.

Three men a dozen or more years older than she were in the waiting room when she returned. They sat with their elbows on the round table, their heads together. Three men in a tub, she thought, but these without discernable employment, kept going by social security and large union pensions, she guessed. Wickes was behind the counter again. "He's refusing to take the breath test," Wickes said when Bridget asked.

"I didn't know you could refuse."

"We can't make someone breathe," Wickes said lightly as if telling a joke. "Wish we could. 'Course with the blood alcohol results we don't need the breath analyzed. It just makes things neater, easier."

"He submitted to a blood test?"

Wickes shrugged.

"I think he should be let go," Bridget said. "Set bail, give him a court date, and let me take him home."

"Doesn't work like that."

"Yes it does. You have to charge him, don't you?"

"Sit down." Wickes pointed at the hard bench.

They did have to charge him, didn't they? She sat on the bench and wished she knew for sure. "Don't they have to charge him?" she asked the sleepy-looking woman beside her. No answer. Either they thought someone did something, or they didn't. Was Myron officially under arrest? She supposed not, not if he had not been charged. But he had been arrested; they both had. Stopped. They had been stopped, and that was the same as arrested, if not in the legal sense, at least in the real sense. Reality seemed a foreigner here. Maybe it was the time. She would have to head out with her choking and whining truck in three hours. The three men were talking now.

"If someone with AIDS bled on this table last night, we could get it just from sitting here," one of them said.

"Right. And if someone with AIDS sat on these chairs before us, we could get it, too. He doesn't have to bleed." Bridget closed her eyes again, but pictured all three of them squirming uncomfortably.

A powerful person would be home by now. His lawyer may be busy still, but he would be sleeping it off, that or rolling around on smooth satin sheets with an attractive garbage woman. Well, Bridget doubted that Myron had a lawyer, but she could only guess. Shouldn't they at least let her send him a message, or let her know he was not being brutalized? They probably had not even told him she was waiting, and he assumed she had abandoned him, left his Buick on Highway 40.

"Tell Myron MacDonald I'm here," she called over to Wickes. "It will cheer him up."

"Sure, Ma'am," Wickes said. "That's what we all want. His cheer." Her eye rolling was so exaggerated this time, her whole head rolled, too.

Bridget rushed up to the counter. "Look!" she said.

"We're busy," Wickes said.

"You are working for me."

"Jeez Louise," Wickes said softly, then sighed. "I'm not working for you. I'm not working for these others." She waved her hand at the room. "I'm not working for your drunken boyfriend. I'm working for the common good."

"There doesn't seem anything good about what you're doing. Any of you. Though you may be common enough." She turned to the three men and the two women. "Stand up for what you need, want, deserve. Whichever. Don't let the police push you around."

They looked at her, all ten eyes, six behind lenses that reflected light, five mouths slightly opened, then turned back to one another, the men continuing their talk. "They just tell us you can only get it from sex," one said.

"Give Myron a message. Let me see him. You must be beating him. Charge him or let him go. Give me a straight answer."

Wickes looked sad and shook her head slowly. "This is not going to be fun," she said.

Bridget jumped up on the counter, sat there with her legs dangling.

"I have to ask you to get down," Wickes said.

"I'm not moving until I get some answers. No. Until I see Myron. He should have been stopped. Sure, I grant you that. But now he should go."

"He's asleep."

"Prove it."

"Get down. Go home."

"I want Myron, I want Myron, I want Myron." She listened to herself chant. Was this Bridget the fun girl, the laughing lassie? Did Myron even remember her last name? She did not have his heart; she had his keys. "I want Myron, I want Myron," she chanted.

"You're going to get in trouble," Wickes said. "You don't want to do this."

"Yes," Bridget said. "I do want to."

"You're as drunk as your boyfriend," Wickes said.

"No. And I'll take your stupid little test. Here." She blew into Wickes's face. "What about it? Have I followed all your little rules? Want me to close my eyes and bring my finger to my nose? Anyone who won't put up with your little evasions must be drunk, is that it?"

Wickes sighed. Bridget saw fatigue and boredom in her face. "It's not me," Wickes said. "I can only tell what I know."

"Listen, I drive a garbage truck," Bridget said, sliding her legs out along the desk top, stretching out on her side, her back to the five others. "Don't try to use the old bureaucratic mess on me as an excuse. My job is more valuable than yours. I, too, have tons of bureaucracy weighing me down, but I manage to pick up the dumpsters on time, all the time." She saw Wickes nod to the young policeman who had come in from the back door. "I want Myron, I want Myron." She slid closer to Wickes, the formica topped counter already hard on her hip and knee. "I want Myron." I don't even know him. She chanted louder. "I want Myron. This is for all of us." She rolled onto her back, faced the acoustic tiles. "This is for the old fools at the table. For Pa and his dead friend Joe. We all want Myron. We want Myron."

When Wickes took hold of one arm, and the other policeman reached across and took hold of the other arm, she did not resist. She allowed herself to be pulled from the counter, to stand on her own on the official side, to be led through a door and down a corridor. Who had the Sublette station route? Even the police station's dumpsters could be *forgotten* for a week or more. Garbage women had power, too. "I want Myron," she said. She considered the double steel doors she was being pulled toward by her grim-faced and silent guards. Were they taking her out the back way, taking her to Myron, taking her to a cell? No matter. She was Bridget Donnelly who daily controlled and tamed a thunderingly powerful machine. Her name meant strength.

THE POET'S DAUGHTER

Kay Larkin is a fixed point in an expanding universe, a stagnant pool beside a waterfall, the air in a windowless room. She is the first little girl tagged, forced to freeze, in a game of statue. Cars, buses, pedestrians move along Cherokee Street beyond the front window of LaBelles' House of Beauty. Kay watches them, cross-eyed at times. She knows at just barely twenty she is not only changeless, but stuck, too, stuck as Beth told her not to be. Of course, her hair changes, and that at least weekly as Horace experiments, making it pink-tinged or asymmetrical. Francis creates; Linus talks; Horace teases, sprays, and rolls; Beth who used to laugh and hug and dance and shake like a wet dog has run away; and even Lamby-pie flutters and shimmies and twitches for Linus. Kay is the wallflower.

Horace is Kay's mother's cousin, the owner of LaBelles' House of Beauty on Cherokee Street in South St. Louis, and her employer. Francis is her father, the mostly unappreciated poet, and Linus is Francis's friend and fellow poet who has yet to finish the epics he discusses. Lamby-pie—no one believes it is her real name, though she insists on it, says her mother just loved her too much—is a dental hygienist who calls herself a poetry groupie. She has her auburn hair cellophaned once a month at LaBelles' and is Linus's latest inspiration. Beth is Kay's mother who has run away, flown the coop, as Francis put it thirteen months ago, running not from Kay, Kay tells herself as she imagines Beth smiling now, even laughing with strangers, shadowy figures who adore her. Sometimes Kay pictures Beth's return, sees her burst through LaBelles' front door, throwing kisses, rushing up to Kay for a hug. Thinking about all of them, those present and the one who has escaped, makes Kay lonelier, a feeling that confuses her as she did not know she was lonely. She does not feel she is anything.

It is late October, 1991, but it may as well be September 4, 1990, the day Kay rushed home from Missouri University to do what she did not know for Francis, inconsolable over Beth's escape he said in his wire. She came to draw close in tragedy, to be part of the comfort and be the comforted at the same time, not believing it possible even then. And she came to pay the bills. She takes care of the trivial parts of living that poets are too sensitive to handle. She thinks idly that all the numbers in her head are what keep her sluggish, make her content to stare through the plastic philodendron leaves in styrofoam under LaBelles' window, content to make appointments and tell the finished products they look like the woman who does the weather on Channel 4, content to listen to Francis and Linus talk about creativity and flowing juices.

She makes six dollars and ten cents an hour at LaBelles' for her thirty-six hours a week: eight to two Mondays and Wednesdays, nine to four Tuesdays and Thursdays, noon to six on Fridays, and eight to one on Saturdays. She earns two hundred and nineteen dollars and sixty cents a week, takes home one seventy-five, sixty-eight; the vitamins Francis has been ordering for ten months that she is supposed to push to Linus and Lamby-pie and others cost sixty-nine twenty-four a month, and so far she sells about thirty dollars' worth; payments on the brick shotgun house a block away are two-twenty a month, ninety of it homeowners' and taxes, with four years to go on the thirty-year loan. Francis's black Ford van, a 1972, was purchased five years ago for three hundred dollars, but needs about five hundred a year in work and an additional one-twenty in insurance and personal property tax. Francis contributes close to one hundred a month collecting cans, but after buying food and gasoline and paying the utilities, Kay has slightly less than one hundred left for emergencies and the great catch-all of Kay's budget, miscellaneous expenses, including clothing and home repairs. Four months ago the city told Kay the sidewalk in front of the brick shotgun had to be made smoother and firmer, which cost more than six hundred, and which she is paying off monthly. When that obligation is over, she imagines, they will need a new furnace. A government loan for her two years at Mizzou is still outstanding, and lately Francis has been saying they need health insurance. One year ago Francis hired a private investigator to find Beth, and though he is still being paid off on the installment plan, his work is finished, his report in: Beth's trail could not be colder.

Kay's bottom lip is chapped and pieces of peeling skin hang from it: she chews on it as she adds and subtracts. When Linus interrupts the litany of expenses, debits and credits, that runs through her mind like a player piano roll, she is almost grateful.

"I'm working on a narrative about good and evil. It takes place on a riverboat with gambling."

"Oh," Kay says. When Beth was still around, Beth would invite Linus to dinner, then nod and smile at his and Francis's talk about truth and creativity and endorphins. Kay imagines Beth's boredom turning to loneliness like her own, imagines Beth, in spite of her ready laughter, feeling diminished by poetic importance. Later Beth would turn on the radio and try to get Francis or Linus to shake and jump with her to songs of their youth. Usually she ended up dancing alone, though sometimes she would grab Kay who mainly stumbled. "At least smile," Beth said to Kay then. "Act like you're having fun, and you will."

Has Beth found someone to twist and shimmy and shout with by now?

Linus rubs his red, bony hands together. "All ready for the reading tonight? Have you heard your dad's latest piece?"

"Unfortunately," Horace says from above and behind the widow Baker as he rolls her perm. "He wanted to practice on me yesterday. I'd rather hear a dramatic reading of the yellow pages."

"Ignore him," Linus says to Kay. "You'll be proud."

" 'The mouse sees, the mouse moves, the mouse is afraid.' I swear that's it." Horace's laugh is small, like hiccuping with a smile. "Terribly moving."

"It's a metaphor," Linus says. "The whole poem is about racial tensions here."

"Oh, poet talk," Horace says. "But Kay is the college girl. I'll let her judge for herself that it's more pretentious but not as important as pigeon poop. First, though, I'll paint shiny strands in her hair, like golden foil."

"Can you do something here, too?" Kay pats the back of her neck as she looks at Horace. "It feels funny. Too thin."

"You need mousse," Mrs. Baker says.

Kay nods. Mrs. Baker is a new widow, and, for the past eight months, everyone's been nodding to her.

"I'll whack it off," Horace says to Kay. When he squirts the setting liquid on Mrs. Baker's pink rollers, Kay turns back to the front window. She tastes the familiar sour milk mixed with vinegar smell by now, tastes it in the back of her throat with each swallow, and she swallows more often with the air so fouled. Horace claims the smell gives him nightmares, but he suffers for commerce, for his three squares and a roof as any good American who is not a Poet with a capital P does. He jokes about his forays into brittle undergrowth or greasy mops. "Once I thought I had struck oil," he told her. "I didn't know whether to comb it or cap it." At twenty-seven he is already slightly stooped from six years of bending over customers' heads, and that, combined with his thinness, his skin so pale it is blue around the mouth, and the baggy black turtlenecks he wears, makes him look to Kay like an existential philosopher, or like one of the poets he ridicules. In fact, his bachelor's degree is in theology, the reason he gives for his atheism.

He and Beth were mainly names to each other, he explains, and claims to have met her three times, tops. "And we, you and I," he says to Kay, "are too distantly related for you to get an inflated blood-is-thicker-than-water kind of salary."

Two hours after Francis's wire—Your Mother Has Flown the Coop Stop I Am Inconsolable Stop Hurry Home—was delivered to Kay's room at Johnston Hall, she was on a Greyhound, headed east. She was two weeks into her third year, majoring in liberal arts, but she left without bothering to withdraw, leaving behind her copies of St. Patrick's Day drinking songs and her popcorn maker. It was like Francis to wire, to shut Kay out with black type on a yellow piece of paper even as he summoned her. A phone call would at least have given her his voice, but it would not have been as dramatic.

Her head hit against the dirty aqua plastic behind it, as the Greyhound in need of shocks bumped and sped down I-70. The stale air made her limbs, even her eyelids, seem heavy and thick. She remembers a yearning. Would Francis have the speech to cross the immeasurable space? Would he talk to her at all?

Kay wrote poems in high school, and one was published in Roosevelt High School's literary magazine, published on a middle page, too, right beside the staples. Her poem was about wrong numbers, a clever metaphor, she still thinks, for isolation. She placed the opened magazine on Francis's desk, the poet's desk, and waited for his praise, his surprise. After a week of his silence, she decided he was disappointed, had found the poem lacking in that essential that makes a poem real.

"About my poem," she said one evening as he stumbled into the living room long after a dinner he had missed.

"Spare me," he said, and plopped down on the scratchy, over-stuffed couch. "I'm past thinking, past talking."

"I just want to know if you liked it. You can nod," she said and sat beside him.

"What?" He closed his eyes and sighed. "You've lost me. Just shut up and give me a hug."

So she did, retrieving her magazine early the next morning, finding it under a pile of pages filled with unconnected words. Of course, it had been about him. He was the wrong number.

Beth used to squeeze when she hugged, as if she and Kay could never be close enough, used to make a sound—ummmm, um—and sway a little before letting go. Beth left because Kay was already gone, Kay told herself, would not have left *her*, would not expect her to return. "You are a dreamer like your father," Beth said once, but Kay did not remember why, did not hear it clearly

enough on the Greyhound to tell whether it was a compliment
or a criticism. The truth was, she seldom looked ahead, imagined
other than what was her life. "You are a poet's daughter," Beth
said. "I never thought I'd have such a quiet child." In the fourth
grade, Kay started laughing loudly and at almost anything. She
forced herself to do so, kept it up for five, six months until Beth
called it an annoying mannerism. It was for you, Kay wanted to
explain, but did not.

✻

"You have to nurture him." Linus is half-sitting on the formica
top of Kay's reception table. He leans close and speaks low as if
what he is saying is new and valuable. "Francis is nervous. He
needs support. His gift is for all of us."

"I support him," Horace says. "I didn't guffaw once when he
read that mouse poem."

"He's working on one about Beth," Linus tells Kay, this time
almost whispering. "It will blow you away." Linus and Francis
met six years ago at the Dry Dock Bar and Grill's open mike night.
They are both poets, although Linus was something else first, has
heard his muse late in life. For a dozen or so years, Linus was in
advertising, where, among other achievements, he orchestrated a
successful light beer campaign. But after receiving advertising's
Man of the Year award, he gave it all up—the fame, the money, and
as a result his wife and child—for poetry, or as Horace told Kay
once, for the romantic idea of the impractical, which to someone
like Linus can appear to be integrity.

"Lamby-pie agrees about the nurturing part," Linus says. "She
says he is getting desperate. Quiet desperation and all that."

Kay moves her heavy head up and down. She thinks Linus's
poems have too much rhyme; in spite of their length they sound
like jingles, jingles repeated over and over. Still, she usually smiles
at him. He looks like Goofy of the Mickey Mouse group, not so
much in his face, which actually does look like a muzzle from the
side, but in the gangling, loose-limbed way he moves, his head
bobbing with each step, his gray ponytail slapping him between
the shoulder blades. Besides, he is her best vitamin customer,

even buying minerals like zinc to keep his feet from smelling and copper to clear his brain. Lamby-pie buys vitamin E because she thinks it improves her sexual performance. Lately, Mrs. Baker has been buying iron, complaining she's tired all the time.

Today Linus needs only vitamin C, and after he leaves with 500 tablets and Mrs. Baker leaves with her iron tablets and looking almost the same as when she entered, Horace and Kay share the sardine and cracker lunch Horace provides, the dead fish smell mixing with the chemicals in the air, almost overpowering that of the setting solution. They lick the oil off their fingers as they eat at Kay's table. Then he cuts her hair straight across the back and adds shimmering gold lines to what is, this week, the color of winter zoysia grass. "It looks like shit," he says when he finishes, "but some fancy pants will believe this is just what she needs to take attention away from a face that seems to be running off like dirt off a car during a downpour."

Kay knows that when Beth was twenty, she was a round-faced, laughing girl, her pink-tinged Irish complexion surrounded by thick, dark curls. Francis has used Beth in many poems as the beautiful maiden, the sprite, and even at forty-five, Beth's age when she ran away, she could have been called a girl. "We're supposed to have only one life before we die," her note said. "But I want two. I loved you and Kay, but I need to fly. I'm tired all the way down to my soul. I'm changing my name and my looks. Enough is enough."

"It was on the kitchen table under the salt shaker," Francis said when Kay read it thirteen months ago. "A strand of her beautiful hair was curled across it."

Kay understands it's luck, the luck of dominant genes lining up in a random order, that make her look like Francis. They both have pinched faces, thin with pointy noses and chins, the color of microwaved chicken. Their brown eyes are too close together, and their mouths too small for the teeth that must jumble up to fit in. They often look embarrassed, Kay as if apologizing for the hair Horace teases and sprays and she wears as a headdress, and they laugh when nothing is funny, when they should be serious, after saying "Grandma had a small stroke," for example, or "the van blew a tire." Kay has noticed this in both of them.

"He doesn't see me because I'm too much like him. I don't stand out," she said to Beth once over a scrambled egg breakfast that Francis, overcome with inspiration, missed. "I'm not sure he knows I'm here. Well, he knows I'm here, but not *me.*"

"Don't worry about what doesn't matter," Beth said. "You think he doesn't know the real you?" She laughed and swung her arm out to the side, pushing the idea away. "The real you is the one you create. That's the fun part."

Kay actually likes Francis's poetry, realizes that liking it places her in a minority. Last Sunday he followed her and the laundry basket to the basement and read as she sorted. His tribute to Beth begins, "I awoke and found you / not wherever I left you / for it was you left me." He is not entirely unpublished; nine pieces have been set in dark type on thick paper in small magazines, university-sponsored journals mainly, and three others have been bootleg-mimeographed at a high school at night, then distributed by a now defunct poetry club. So it is twelve in all, nine of them true bright spots, moments of hope in twenty-two years of rejection. The most recent reason for hope came three years ago when the *Downtown Review* took two at a time. "Poets never are recognized anyway," Beth used to say. "They do it because they like it. No one reads poetry."

Kay once told a date, a tall blond who took her to Roosevelt's junior prom, that Francis was a salesman, and rationalized it was true every now and then when he took jobs selling encyclopedias, vacuum cleaners, or basement waterproofing systems. One summer he sold ice cream at a local drive-in. She told her roommate at Johnston Hall her father was self-employed, deciding can collecting was a distinctly American cottage industry. Lying, bending and twisting reality so it could just as well have been so, has come easily. "It's okay," she has said to him. "If I had a new coat I would just look like all the other girls." Or "but I really honestly and truly do not like amusement parks." He accepted her protestations each time, just as he did Beth's. "I'll take your word for it," he would say. "It's all you have."

Oh, she thinks, he did apologize for not being able to send her to college, not even to the state school, but as she thinks it, she knows it is not true, not a memory. Beth did the apologizing. She used the usual words: "your father and I," and "my salary," and "I've heard about loans." Then Beth added, "just so you're going away," and "not to learn responsibility or because Columbia, Missouri, has anything to offer, but for the going. To know you can, to know you're not stuck."

The reading that evening is at Junkarama, a relatively new self-styled bohemian hang-out on Pestalozzi Street a few blocks north of Cherokee. It is in the first floor of a turn-of-the-century red brick building that has once been condemned, and its upstairs still is. The three owners, former high school teachers, decorate it with old tires, rusted fenders, empty wine bottles with colored candle wax melted down them, wheelbarrows without wheels, televisions without screens, and whatever else they can scrounge from junkyards and the basements of their friends. It is a theme place. One of the owners is a painter who works in oil on old cabinet and refrigerator doors and large pieces of plywood. In a flat, primitive style, he depicts the violent crimes he reads of in the newspapers, the more sadistic and macabre the better. His work is displayed and for sale.

Horace says gimmicky places like Junkarama give him a pain, make him despair of humans ever getting to the heart of anything. According to him the only places with a right to longevity are the corner bars full of bloated men and heavy-bottomed women in rose-colored stretch pants singing Sinatra songs, drinking Budweiser, and discussing Father Schultz's sermon of the week before—"Imagine his saying war is un-Christian." Horace says those are real people, not quick to follow trends, though he admits that allowing Catholics to drink does not make them more sophisticated than Baptists, just louder. Kay can almost hear Beth, the semifallen Catholic, laughing at that.

But as long as Junkarama survives, Francis and Linus and anyone else who cares to can read poems or otherwise perform on the weekends to a handful of customers who nurse their drinks all night and to the two women, mother and daughter in matching straw sailors with broken brims, who live at the nearby bus stop.

For Francis's performance, Kay wears what she has decided will be her reading attire, a gray nubby sweater discarded by Francis years ago and white tights. Her hair feels a foot high, and though she swings her head, the newly golden-streaked curls alongside her face are motionless. This week, Horace wants to bring 1965 back, says it may be his claim to fame. Francis waves her over when she enters, waves extravagantly with large swoops of both arms as if she could lose him in the crowd, a handful of people scattered among the six round varnished-yellow tables. Francis is at the center table with Linus and Lamby-pie in her white hygienist's pantsuit, and another poet Kay has met before, a short, stocky man who answers to both Clay and Shay.

"I was afraid you wouldn't make it," Francis says. "It's about time to start."

Kay pats his arm and sits to his right. She has never missed a reading, just as she has never missed telling him he is great. Lately, she has never missed paying a bill. The bus-stop women are sitting at the table beside the stage, eating Cheerios out of a paper bag. At the table between them and Kay are three skinny young men, college students, Kay thinks. They slouch in their chairs, yet look around too often, trying to spot the poet. Likely they consider themselves poets, too.

A man about Linus and Francis's age, a businessman perhaps, in a navy blue blazer, enters and sits by himself near the door. He places his briefcase on the table, and when his dark golden liquid in a short glass arrives, he rests it on the worn-looking leather. Francis points him out to Kay. Perhaps he has been sent by the mayor who was invited personally because some poems in Francis's repertoire are about St. Louis, about its racial problems. "Art can and should make a difference," Francis says. "Change us."

"You, my friend, are the reporter," Linus says, raising his can of beer to Francis. "The chronicler of our times, the troubadour."

"Oh." Lamby-pie twitters like a sparrow. "Aren't we impressed."

Odd, Kay thinks but knows she will not say, that the whole crowd, such as it is, is white so-called, Caucasian so-called. Perhaps that speaks about racial tension more than the poem. Instead she smiles and pats the poet's arm again. Somewhere, not even a block away, are people who do not know poets. For more than a year, Beth has had a whole other life.

At eight-thirty, after downing two plastic tumblers of Chablis in twenty minutes to calm himself, Francis takes his place at the microphone, which, like much of what is in Junkarama, does not work. Nevertheless, Francis clears his throat and speaks into the mike. "What We Fear," he begins, but is interrupted in the middle of his second line. One of the owners, not the painter but the one who has been taking drink orders, comes from the kitchen through the swinging door to announce that an old electric toaster oven is now working. He is wearing a white chef's apron stained red and yellow and meant for a shorter person. It hits him midthigh. He has rewired the toaster oven himself, he explains, and is able to offer individual pizzas or some special miniature frozen hamburgers he is dying to try. The college boys order pizzas, and Linus orders burgers for Kay and Clay and Lamby-pie. The owner smiles and bows at each order, then turns to Francis and salutes. "You're on, Larkin. Go to it."

Francis reads his first poem, "What We Fear," then one about a dark-haired nymph who stole his heart, one about flowers or death or both, and one about litter. While Francis reads, the owner listens from the kitchen and writes out checks to his many creditors and waits to hear the burgers sizzle. But the tape around the wire splicing does not hold, has not covered the wires well in the first place, is the wrong kind of tape. The reports later are conflicting. Nevertheless, first one, then two sparks shoot out with pops and crackles the owner should hear, would have too if he were not so intent on adding a column of figures over and over to get the same answer twice. The sparks fall on the splintered grease-soaked wood that forms the countertop. Soon there are flames, flames that move down the cabinets and across the wooden floor covered with old throw rugs. The owner calls the fire department and throws glasses of water on the flames while he waits.

Francis begins his best poem, "The mouse sees . . ."

Kay has stopped listening long ago. She studies the scene, her father, the others, with crossed eyes and discovers she can make the yellow of the tabletop move closer and fall back by tightening her eye muscles. She tries it on the gory works, and makes one of a prostitute's decapitation—fountains of red, red blood spouting from her neck—move on the wall. The sirens only add to the distortion around her. Francis stops after three lines, yells that he will wait for the sirens to pass. Lights race around the room, red and white circles chase one another across the walls and ceiling, skip from a varnished table to the pictures of death. Two firemen enter dragging a hose, and four more follow them into the kitchen. Another stands with a megaphone, ordering an evacuation.

"No," Francis says. "I'm not finished. This is my best."

"This is a fire," the fireman says into the megaphone, at Francis, not ten feet from him. "People as stupid as you die in fires."

"Philistine," Francis says.

✳

"Ridiculous," Francis says the next morning over his Cream of Wheat. "Ridicu-fucking-lous. Don't you think? It's a sham. A travesty. A curse. Come on, tell me what you think of it."

"You need a hug," she says.

"We always fall short. Nothing is enough. I need more than that. I need to be published, better published. I need a book. Then I would not have to spend my time at garbage place like Junkarama, junk places like garbagarama." He throws his spoon across the table, hitting the salt shaker. His face glows red for a moment, then turns splotchy. A temperamental tantrum. "I should be established by now. I need recognition, need to be established."

Don't confuse need and want is the refrain Kay grew up to, with. Beth said it when Kay wanted money to buy doll clothes or cellophane wrapped cupcakes or cassette tapes of groups her friends liked. "We are not poor," Beth said. "If we were, we wouldn't have a home or food or clothes. Hell, we even have a frost-free refrigerator. You don't need more, not what you think you need but really just want. Knowing the difference can keep you from sadness, keep you bounding out of bed each morning ready to cartwheel to evening."

Kay heard that familiar speech in the stores where the want was strongest while she stood before the unattainable objects of desire. It must have been that way, her childhood, because that is how she remembers it, yet she knows it may not have been. She wishes as usual that she had a sister or a brother or both who would have lived through the same time with different memories, who may remember calling Beth *Mom* or remember Beth gazing into the distance, perhaps watching airplanes long after they disappeared into the sky, remember Beth poised for escape. Kay may have missed many clues, may have looked away at the important moments, crossed her eyes.

Maybe wants could change into needs, just as they could disappear from neglect.

"All my life," Francis says now, pounding the table with his fist for emphasis, "I've done my best to keep things in perspective, to write *and* be around my family, trying not to be discouraged when no-talent fools were published over me, when I saw publishers were afraid to take a chance on real art, jealous perhaps, determined to keep the same pap and drivel in print. Am I rewarded? Not that I expected it, but am I? No. My wife runs away, my daughter quits school, and my poems are ignored. I do better selling vitamins."

No. Kay almost says no; the vitamins are the worst. She has shown him before—all it takes is subtracting what they make each month on Linus and the few others from what they pay to the California company that sells in bulk. They lose almost forty dollars a month, but Francis seems unable to grasp it. "Poets can neither add nor subtract," Beth said more than once when Kay was innocent enough to think it a joke, to chuckle politely, for it never was a funny joke. Francis says if they lose only forty or so, they are succeeding, they will catch on. Now Kay tells him the same about himself. He will catch on. She crosses to his side of the table and rubs his back, sliding her hands over his ribs, and tells him the main family joke. Artists have to suffer. He is too good not to succeed, that one not exactly a joke, more like the family mantra.

She pictures herself living in France, Nice perhaps, or living in Lubbock, Texas, or maybe Botswana. They are visions rather than plans, revelations as sudden as the Blessed Mother must have been to the children of Fatima. Why not go to Fatima? Horace would know about visions. So would Beth, Kay knows, whose wants must have involved geography even as they did not include Kay.

✳

For four days, Francis paces the house, taking giant strides from the stove all the way to the living room picture window, passing through his and her bedrooms on the way up and back. He stops by LaBelles' during the day and paces the reception area. "Gee, Cuz-in-law," Horace says rubbing his nonexistent beard with his hand. "Is something lodged in your artistic little brain? Sit down. You're scaring the customers."

"Lamby-pie and I hope Francis doesn't throw in the towel," Linus says one afternoon as he sits in the reception area and waits for Lamby-pie to be combed out.

"Why should he?" Kay asks.

"I could just weep like a willow at the thought," Lamby-pie says, her voice sounding almost southern. "First your darlin' mother leaves, and now he may be ready to quit, a broken man." Later, though, Kay hears the usual St. Louis nasal tones, the flat vowels, as Lamby-pie talks to Horace. "The sticker price means zilch. It's the options that count," she says.

New numbers already clutter Kay's brain. She has found out that a bus ticket to Memphis is eighty dollars, and she has that much. She guesses a month's rent in a small room in the worst part of town is about two hundred, and maybe she can find someone who will not make her pay in advance. When she goes, she will take some food, but still will have to spend about fifty the first month, even if she eats mainly rice and bouillon. She will have to find a job immediately but can always wait tables or work in a shop like LaBelles', as she does have experience. She will do like Beth and change her name. Horace changes her appearance every few days anyway. She will go to Memphis because it is one of the cheapest tickets available, and she will leave on a Saturday evening, perhaps the upcoming one, because Horace won't miss her until Monday at 8 A.M. Francis will miss her, she knows, sooner if she leaves a note which she will not do, if she calls attention to her absence as Beth did. Kay will leave the cases of vitamins. If she were to leave a note, it would say love in the past tense, would include, like Beth's note, the piercing *d.*

"He could publish himself," Linus says, cracking the knuckles on his right hand one at a time. "There is no real shame in it."

Kay shrugs. It is Thursday, and she may as well go this Saturday. One is like the other. She will change, become unstuck, in just two days. She will not talk to poets in Memphis.

That night the familiar nightmare, the one she had in the first few months after Beth's break-out, returns. Kay is lying on her stomach, and is awakened by something heavy and alive on her back, clinging. She feels the wind go out of her from the force of its landing. It is warm and breathes in her ear. She does not move. She cannot tell if it is human or another kind of animal, but after a while it starts to growl, a deep rumbling noise full of evil intent, a threat, a warning for her to lie perfectly still. She does, knowing, because the dream is recycled, that the thing will eventually leave without harming her. She has only to pretend not to exist. This time, though, it is different. She wakes up completely and discovers *she* is growling. For a moment, though awake, she cannot stop. When she does, she hears Francis moving in the dark, still doing his tormented dance, she thinks, his walk for pity and woe. She reminds herself to tell him again how much she likes his mouse poem.

She sees the note, propped against the Cream of Wheat box, as soon as she enters the kitchen. It is long and rambling, consciously important with pronouncements about art and life. She knows he expects her to save it, perhaps after dripping one or two poignant, poetic tears for auld lang syne in the margins so as not to blur the words. She is to be proud and invigorated by his refusal not to let the bastards get him down, he says, and will surely understand his need for "new vistas to spark new visions." He wants her to know he is not leaving because of her. No. Of course not. She is incidental once again. She tears his excuse in two, then in two again. She wonders how he will pay his bills, who will pay, knows he will find someone. She retrieves Beth's note from the string and tape and appliance warranty drawer where Francis filed it, and tears it as well. She tears until she has confetti, then convinces herself she is too old to be an orphan. Anyway, family is a want, not a need. She will tell Horace she needs her light brown color back, and if Linus, Lamby-pie, or even old Joe Baker's sad widow try to comfort her, she'll laugh and laugh as Beth used to, as loud as she can.

HENRIETTA

Henrietta Marschand was not, in the giving and self-sacrificing sense, a nice woman; and indeed, had never in all of her eighty-five years tried to please someone other than herself, unless of course it was convenient for her as well, or unless it was her only son Henry who had paid her back, when he returned from the war in Korea boys his age fought, by marrying a woman so dumb she thought Angola was a type of sweater. No, if given the chance—and one always was—Henrietta chose herself. And that made sense to her, seemed natural and smart. She was as good as anyone else, after all, and better than most. She had usually entertained and interested some others, thus doing her bit for the human race. Besides, she had seldom hurt anyone, that is, not on purpose, just for the hurting.

In fact, every now and then Henrietta felt positively saintly, and knew that was partly because she lived in a virtually germ- and dirt-free apartment in South St. Louis next to Holy Cross Catholic Church, and mainly because it was easier to be a saint at eighty-five than it had been at twenty-five, or forty-five, or even sixty-five. And she was a sweet-looking woman who knew it, counted on it when she asked the man at the market across the street to help her with her bags, when she used to get Joe Baker who ran the produce store to save her the largest avocado, when she waited for younger men (and older ones if she saw any) to open doors for her, when she expected to be offered one of the two armchairs in her internist's waiting room. Her hair, at one time so black it was blue and shiny from the egg she washed it with once a week, was white and, though thin, still had enough body that Horace at LaBelles' House of Beauty two blocks away could get it to curl in around her face. And her face was smooth, smooth as a peach, Joe Baker used to say, smoother than the faces of any of the other women in her senior citizen apartment building, even those just barely seventy. And her voice was not weak, quavery, like most others, and her eyesight was better than she had a right to expect; even from fifteen pews back, she could see Father Mullamphy's lips move as he read what used to be called the Confiteor.

She missed that crazy priest, wished he were still around to liven up the predictable services. She had had to stifle a laugh when he stood at the end of the casket and talked about Joe Baker. "The sucker principle," he had said, and Joe only three days dead. She was in church the morning a few months later when the crazy priest started telling all the sins he knew and had to be taken away. She was thankful, then, that she had not been stupid enough to confess to one so clearly unbalanced. Of course, the pity was that old women like her seldom had anything to confess, surely not anything evil or exciting enough to repeat.

Take old Ruth Eisle up there at the lectern, reading from the Book of Kings. She couldn't see well enough to tell *dominion* from *domination*, couldn't speak clearly enough anyway to keep from sounding like a radio you were almost out of range of, was an insult to those like Henrietta who took the trouble to get up early and come to mass, and who would have offered her still strong and full voice for the epistle had she known there was a need. She had despised Ruth, been plagued by Ruth, for what seemed forever, for most of what the insurance brochures called her sunset years, but it had begun long before.

When Ruth's husband, Ted, had taken a job as ticket taker on the passenger train and made the run from St. Peters to St. Louis, stopping at Union Station—now a shopping mall—and staying overnight three nights in an inexpensive downtown hotel, that had not been Henrietta's fault. And the fact that Henrietta's husband of less than three years operated one of the fruit stands in Union Station, and that Henrietta herself with her dimples and all that black hair hanging down her back sold Ted an apple each time he passed as he made jokes about Eve and temptation until she had to join him in his hotel room after her husband left her in the evenings to visit his widowed mother was not Henrietta's fault either. If Otis, the husband, had stayed home, if his mother had not been both ill and clinging, if Henrietta had not been beautiful, if Ted had not been that kind of man, and if poor silly Ruth had been a more exciting woman, nothing would have happened. And nothing very much did happen, either: just a little flattery and flirting, some time spent with Ted brushing her long hair, and then quick sex, which she liked for the urgency and speed, until the time she decided she may rather have Ted than Otis all the time, and Ted laughed.

"I don't think my wife would go for that," he said, and began to talk about Ruth, showering her with loving testimonials, calling her a "real feminine woman," "a true partner," "a terrific mother for the light of our lives, Charlene," all of which made Henrietta mean, mean enough to write to Ruth, General Delivery, St. Peters, Missouri, thirty miles away, and tell all.

Well, Henrietta did not and had not considered the sex immoral, no matter what the Church taught—though she confessed anyway as soon as it was clear that Ted had transferred to another route, and so her near occasion of sin was gone. And she did not consider it wrong to sneak out, deceive dear Otis like that. He was a sweet boy, though quiet and boring, and if she had not loved him, she would not have married him. She had had many other offers. His college failure was to blame. Before he went to Washington University on a full-tuition scholarship, he had been a flirt, laughing and teasing all the girls, and she knew the prestige she enjoyed for being the prettiest was enhanced by his choosing her. After only two years of college, though, he flunked out but left the best part of him behind. He was a mild-mannered failure whose head bowed over his slumped shoulders more and more each year. Sure, he still loved her, but as if she were an old friend of the family rather than his main heartthrob. She had watched in confusion as his desires evaporated slowly during his college years. Nevertheless, she was his wife, and had he wanted her in that way often, she would have stayed home. As she saw it, he had dibs on her. But as it turned out, she took nothing from him that he wanted. Nor did she think it was wrong because of Ted, for he was certainly not the victim and had known all along what he was about.

But it had been wrong to write to Ruth, probably immoral, surely cruel. Henrietta had known it then, and she knew it now, but the letter from Ruth was mean, too, was a way of rubbing Henrietta's nose in her own wrongness. "I'm praying for you," Ruth wrote in red ink on pink stationary. "We weak human beings need both strength and forgiveness. I pray for us all." Then the Christmas card later that year from Ted, Ruth, Charlene, and Henrietta (the French poodle Ruth had recently given Ted for his birthday) made Henrietta wish for the collapse of the bridge over the Missouri River and the permanent isolation of St. Peters from civilized society.

And now as punishment for her sins, Henrietta walked home from daily mass with Ruth, helping Ruth by holding her steady when she felt faint on extremely humid days and by guiding her in winter down the cleared narrow path in the sidewalk. "Be careful. Step where I do," she said as she did this morning, because with her poor vision, Ruth was just as likely to step on a patch of ice as not. As Henrietta helped and befriended Ruth, she considered it a penance stiffer than the Our Fathers the priests gave in confession, a reparation for her whole life, a way of racking up points toward her own salvation. At eighty-five, it was not too early to start storing up indulgences and good marks for eternity.

"It's going to be a cold one," Ruth said now as they walked the half-block to their building.

"I'm surprised," Henrietta said, "that after living eighty-seven years in the Midwest, you still consider the cold of January worthy of comment. You act like it's a news flash."

"We should live in Hawaii. Laura was there for two weeks, and she said she slept with her windows open every night," Ruth said. "What a wonderful trip she had, too." Laura was Charlene's eldest daughter, and Henrietta often heard about Laura's travels, promotions, experiences. No matter where Laura went, even if just to a high school play one of her children (Ruth's great-grandchildren) was in, it was the best place possible, was exceptional. Henrietta, on the other hand, spoke to her own granddaughter, Patsy, when Patsy wanted to borrow money to get another degree, go to another school to become a licensed insurance salesperson, business manager, or preschool aide. Henrietta always said no, too, but not without a lecture that included telling Patsy to get rid of the bum she was living with, the so-called freelance artist who claimed he was trying to get jobs but never did. "When you were twenty, you preached to me about freedom and love," Henrietta usually said. "Now that you're beyond forty, I hope you see that hard work and sacrifice and goals are more important."

"The mayor of Honolulu is a friend of theirs, you know," Ruth was saying as they entered the overly heated lobby. "Of course, he's loaded. His family had money, I think. But anyway, Laura said they stayed with him, and he had a great big place on the ocean with three floors and wings and whatnot. It had whatchacallit, thirty-foot ceilings, and one wall was glass from top to bottom."

"No one knows what whatchacallit is, and if you have to babble, at least babble about people I know." Henrietta knew that if she could only manage to be civil to Patsy, she wouldn't have to listen to Ruth, only Ruth, ad nauseam.

"Her husband didn't go with her at first, even though the mayor is his friend from the Navy. Laura went by herself and her husband joined her later because his mother is sick. She's a Garner, you know."

"Who is? I don't know any Garners."

"A cousin of the Garners who live on Delor, I think. Anyway, she's in terrible shape with strokes and blood clots, and now she's being fed by tubes through her nose. That's the only way. But Laura stayed two weeks and she said he had a white grand piano, the mayor did, and he would play it at night, and he's just a card, I guess. A real kidder. So one night, he was playing. This was when Laura's husband was there, so it must have been near the end. And he put his hands whatchacall on his head and kept playing. He had made it into a player, see? Well, Laura said that was really something. They all got a big kick out of that."

"Why would anyone want to be fed through the nose?" Henrietta said. "I mean it, Ruth." She was concerned about the so-called advances in medicine, had been for a while. A ninety-year-old from the apartment had had a foot amputated recently so she could live another two months, not long enough to learn to handle her wheelchair. After that, Henrietta had made both Patsy and Ruth swear on the Bible that they would not let her be cut up, end up with tubes in all kinds of odd places, not dead, but not too alive, either. Not that Patsy, the proclaimed atheist, cared about the Bible, but Ruth took it seriously. And Ruth would likely be around, be the one to decide. "Don't call the paramedics and have them start pumping my chest," Henrietta had told Ruth. "Just close my eyes."

Ruth shrugged out of her coat, draped it over one arm, and presented her back to Henrietta. "Unzip me," she said. "I'm going up and take this dress off. Charlene always buys me dresses that zip up the back, and I don't know why."

Henrietta unzipped Ruth's dress, and Ruth walked slowly into the elevator, displaying an expanse of damp, white skin. "Are you coming?" Ruth asked. "Yesterday, I forgot to press four, so I rode up to eight and back again, twice, before I remembered." She laughed. "But then, it's not like I'm in a hurry."

"You give me a thumping headache," Henrietta said. "I think I'll sit down here alone. Maybe I'll call Charlene and tell her you need a keeper."

The apartment building they lived in was not a nursing home, but was exclusively for senior citizens, those fifty-five and older. Henrietta was saddened whenever she realized if Henry were still alive, he would be eligible, would, in fact, have been eligible for ten years. But Henry had died of a heart attack while playing tennis in Forest Park with Joe Baker. Henry was just Patsy's age then, forty-two, the father of a nineteen-year-old, Patsy, and on his way to becoming wealthy through his food brokerage business. But he had been burdened by a money-crazed wife, one who was not satisfied even with the Persian lamb coat and the Thunderbird, one who also wanted a condo at the Lake of the Ozarks. It was common knowledge that stress caused heart attacks, and living with Tricia, whose attitude Henrietta described as slightly more selfish than "gimmee gimmee," had to have been stressful.

Nevertheless, the senior citizen apartment was perfect for Henrietta, a woman who liked her privacy but had begun to fear living in a separate house. She no longer had to triple-bolt her doors or put bars on her windows to guard against the horror the television and newspapers convinced her was rampant. And though there was no nursing care, the residents watched out for and checked up on one another, ready to push the help buttons— two in each apartment—that would bring the EMS teams. But, of course, Henrietta knew everything was okay only as long as the buttons were not pushed. She had even petitioned unsuccessfully to have hers disconnected. She knew she would never use them.

She and Ruth had come to the apartment building together, moved in within weeks of each other three years ago. Sixty-three years earlier when Ted said good-bye to Henrietta and she and Ruth had been only types to each other—one the wicked other woman, and one a drab and lifeless mother-of-the-year—neither would have thought they'd be spending their old age together. Ted surely would get a hoot out of it, Henrietta told herself often, but he had died of stomach cancer so many years ago, almost thirty, and besides, she remembered him so little, she wasn't sure he even had a sense humor.

Henrietta finally left the lobby, noticing that just standing and walking to the elevator tired her more than usual. She should rest for a while, take a nap before lunch. Or she could skip lunch altogether. Today was meat loaf, never good.

From her apartment on the seventh floor, through the sliding glass door that opened to a narrow balcony, she could see the house she and Otis had lived in, the one he had died in while sitting at the dinner table when only fifty years old, falling face down into the apple cobbler. And afterwards she stayed in that house because Henry and his family, including three-year-old Patsy, lived a few blocks away. She stayed until the late sixties, until Henry was dead, too, and the neighborhood filled up with people who put fake wood paneling on the tall, cool plaster walls, lowered the ten-foot ceilings, boarded up and bricked over the fan lights and transoms and stained glass windows, put aluminum siding over the bricks, and put Astroturf on the front stoops. It was what she told Patsy amounted to hoosier remodeling. And once a neighborhood was full of hoosiers, women with rollers in their hair who scream, "Get your ass in here," at their children, who soon learn to shout vulgarities also, the others, the ones Patsy told her then to call blacks, with their beat-up cars and loud radios, would be next.

So she moved west in the direction of St. Peters, but south of that to an area of instant neighborhoods and luxury town-houses. She bought a luxury townhouse, and Patsy helped her settle in, but refused, she said the whole time, to condone her grandmother's urban flight. "I guess I can live anywhere I want," Henrietta said. "I've saved my money for nice things, and now I have this kitchen with a dishwasher and an icemaker. Besides," she added to make Patsy angry, "I'm not fleeing anything worth saving. Hoosiers comb their hair in public."

The year she moved into her townhouse with plush rust-colored carpet and central air, the year she decided she did not miss cracked plaster and foot-wide baseboards that always needed dusting or painting or both, was the year Patsy took up with that artist. No doubt about it, Henrietta thought now as she looked out at the television antenna of her old house, Patsy and the artist had been together a long time, twenty-three years so far, just as Patsy had predicted. "We are committed," she had said at the beginning. "Even without a piece of paper." Still, if the artist ever sold anything, got any kind of job at all, Henrietta knew he would be gone. Patsy supported him and was being taken for a ride. When she got to be fifty or so, the artist would find a younger woman. Especially since Patsy refused to wear makeup, was letting the gray stay in her brown hair. That was the way it worked. Henrietta wondered why she couldn't make Patsy see that she wasn't concerned about all that living-in-sin business; it was the stupidity of her own kin she couldn't take.

It was her first Christmas in the townhouse that the artist gave her a pen-and-ink sketch of her old home with its mansard roof and double-doored entrance. It was Christmas Eve when they brought it over, grinning like idiots, overly pleased with themselves for bearing the perfect gift, and Henrietta had said, "What's it supposed to be of?" Then to let them know she did not approve of their arrangement, did not recognize the artist as a person with a right to give her anything, she told them to take it home. And that was that. She spent her holidays alone for a while until Ruth started insisting she join her at Charlene's, or in later years, at Laura's. And even then, Henrietta fixed her own holiday dinner and ate it beforehand because, as she told Ruth over and over, neither Charlene nor Laura could earn their livings as cooks, not even for the bums who ate at the Salvation Army mission downtown.

Henrietta met Ruth at the first bingo party she attended at that fancy new church in West County that looked like a bank, and when Ruth recognized her name, Henrietta said, "How's the poodle?"

"If you want to fight," Ruth said, "let's do it in private. Come over for lunch tomorrow. Ted's dead, and I want to protect his name in public."

At lunch the next day, in Ruth's equally luxurious new town-house, over chicken salad with too much mayonnaise, Ruth graciously forgave Henrietta, acted the victorious woman who had held on to her man, placed Henrietta in the category of also-ran. "He chose as I knew he would," Ruth said. "He and I had a strong bond. It could survive minor temptations."

It was too much for Henrietta to take. "I could have had Ted if I'd wanted him," she said. She pushed her plate to the side. "We had fun. Have you ever wondered how much? Have you ever, in your whole boring life I mean, had fun, real fun?" She tried briefly, but could not remember any fun, could not remember Ted's face anymore. "If you had been better, he wouldn't have strayed. Your mother should have told you that before you were married." She stood, picked up her purse and the beige gloves no one but her wore anymore. "I doubt Ted ever had much of a good name, though he did have a reputation on his route. And I do not want to be your friend."

But Ruth was hard to insult. When Henrietta was down with the Hong Kong flu a few months later, Ruth brought soup, aspirin, hot toddies, and Henrietta was grateful initially but annoyed later, annoyed mainly that Ruth had realized she had no one else. Henrietta had not spoken to Tricia since long before her move, since Tricia had talked Henry into selling the business he had inherited from Otis, the food brokerage business that had begun as a fruit stand that Henrietta had worked her fanny off in. And Henry, out of misplaced loyalty, had stopped all but the basic communication with his own mother a few years before his death. And for so many years, Patsy had been busy marching for Civil Rights, Women's Rights, Gay Rights, whatever, and when Henrietta reminded her she was a troublemaker and should earn some money and dump the artist, Patsy would sulk and stay away until she wanted money.

When Henrietta was sixty-seven, four years after her move to the new parish, she was accused of not turning in all the bingo profits. She had been a card seller for most of the four years. Ruth defended her, even when it was clear to all that Henrietta had been paying herself, as she admitted, just a few dollars an evening. "After all," she said. "I am not one to steal, but if the Catholic Church is so concerned with justice and charity, why would it expect me to work on Saturdays and Wednesdays for nothing?"

"That's exactly right," Ruth had said to those, including the pastor, who wanted to bar Henrietta from all future games. "Henrietta has always done only what she thought right." And at that, Henrietta told Ruth to shut up, told the priest she was quitting her bingo job, and tried to insult him by saying he and Ruth were two of a kind: simple-minded and ugly.

Still, Ruth remained loyal and true, remained Henrietta's only friend, and when it was time to move again, this time into an easier-to-handle place, Henrietta chose the old neighborhood, one where she could walk to church and to the market, and she told Ruth about her choice. Ruth put her name on the senior citizen apartment's waiting list even before Henrietta did, sold her townhouse before Henrietta sold hers, and lucked into one of the nicer corner apartments above the quiet street. "Why, oh Lord," Henrietta prayed, "am I so cursed?"

As Henrietta was unzipping her own dress, reminding herself she was not nearly as decrepit as Ruth was, there was a knock, and then, as none of the residents locked their doors, hers opened. "Grandma?" Patsy asked. "Are you here?"

"Where would I be?" Henrietta asked. "Why are you here?"

"I wanted to see you."

"You should have called first. I'm tired."

"Thank you. I'd love to sit," Patsy said, and did. "And it's great to see you, too."

"You want money," Henrietta said, and zipped herself back up. "How much?"

"How much will you give?"

"Nothing."

"How much will you lend then?"

Henrietta sat, too, and put her feet up on the coffee table, an act she considered a prerogative of age. She no longer had to protect her furniture, keep it good indefinitely. "At my age, I don't make loans." Her age! It wasn't impossible that she would outlive Patsy, but eighty-five was pushing it. If her body would only cooperate, she'd go forever. She often thought her eighty-five years a trick, a lie she almost fell for. She thought of herself as sixtyish. "Do me a favor," she said. "Do something for me, and I may do something for you."

"Here's a question," Patsy said. "Am I in your will?"

"Hello," Ruth said and entered the small living room before Henrietta could answer Patsy. "Can you give me a zip? I'm going down to lunch."

"Why don't you keep your clothes on for a whole day?" Henrietta asked as she started to stand.

"I'll do it," Patsy said. She stood and Ruth presented her back. "I'm Patsy. I know you're Ruth."

"What a lovely surprise your visit must be."

"What makes you think it's a surprise?" Henrietta asked, and eased herself back into the couch cushions.

"I've heard a lot about you," Patsy said to Ruth. She smoothed the shoulders of Ruth's dress once it was zipped. It was a blue-and-white check, not the dress she had worn that morning, and Henrietta knew why. Ruth wore it to lunch because it was relatively new and some old fool who had not yet seen it might comment, and Ruth would be able to puff up like a refrigerator biscuit and say her darling granddaughter Laura gave it to her. Henrietta had already given Ruth her opinion of the dress: the color blue made the liver spots on Ruth's face stand out that much more. It was the truth.

"If it wasn't a surprise, you'd have told me," Ruth said.

"I don't tell you everything. Go down and show off your dress."

"It's a nice dress," Patsy said. "A good color on you."

"Too bad she can't work zippers," Henrietta said.

"You look fresh and energetic," Ruth said to Patsy. "Is that what you wear to work?"

"I just bought this," Patsy said, stepping back to give Ruth a better view of her shiny red leotard covered below the waist by a black wrap-around skirt.

"Ha!" Henrietta said. "She can't keep a job. Just one pig-in-the poke after the other. She's here for my money."

"I'm a new aerobics exercise instructor. Started yesterday. It's a real forty-hour-a-week job."

"Laura has a friend who teaches exercise classes. A man. One she almost married years ago, but she wasn't really in love with him, not like she is with her husband. He lives in Denver—the exercise teacher, not the husband."

"The favor you can do for me, in case you've forgotten, is to grow up." Henrietta spoke to Patsy, but she looked straight ahead, through the glass door at the television antenna on her old house, shining in the winter sun. "I want you to act as if you have some sense, as if you take after your father instead of your mother. At least make him marry you. One day, you'll be left with nothing." Her own words echoed in her head. She could not tell if she was speaking too loud or not loud enough. "And Ruth, no one wants to hear about Laura's friends or Hawaii. Patsy wants to know if she's in my will."

"Denver," Ruth said.

"Am I, Grandma? Because if I am, I thought I may as well use some of it now when it could help me get a start. I want to buy into the exercise corporation."

"A start! You're forty-two."

"It's never too late, right Ruth?"

"Ask your rich mother for money," Henrietta said.

"I don't speak to people who wear dead animals," Patsy said. "I wouldn't stoop so low."

"Just as low as me, huh? Just low enough to torment me, to steal from me, to anticipate my death." She stood suddenly, as quickly as she had when she was a young, supple girl with swinging and shining hair, a girl with a twenty-inch waist who could touch her toes and do backflips with the boys from the train bridge into the Meramec River. The room darkened, and her left arm jerked. "I never did anything so horrible to you that you have to smack your lips at the thought of my death. And if I did, I'm not a bit sorry. I am going to do my best to spend all my money before I go. I would hate like hell to leave you any." She sank back down and closed her eyes.

After a few moments of silence, Ruth said she was going down to lunch, and then did. Patsy remained standing above Henrietta, looking down at her pitiful grandmother. Henrietta knew it without opening her eyes. Anger and hatred and meanness were diminished by age. To the young they became sad or cute or, at most, irritating eccentricities.

"Bye, Grandma," Patsy finally said, and Henrietta whispered, "good riddance."

Considering all, it had not been much of a life. Pathetic and sad Otis, weak Henry, stupid Patsy, chowder-brained Ruth. A beautiful and strong and smart woman should have had a better ride. With her eyes still closed, she saw her future clearly. There was no other one possible. The oaths and promises notwithstanding, Ruth would push the help button, call the paramedics. Henrietta would be fed through a tube; veins would be taken from her thighs and placed in her arms just for the feeding. Or perhaps she'd be fed through her nose. Balloons would invade her spaces. She would end up staring into the face that fluffed her pillow, not knowing if it belonged to someone she should remember or to a paid attendant. She could hear Ruth now, hear the answer she would make about the call to the paramedics when her own judgment day arrived. Surely God would wonder why the oath was taken in vain.

"Oh my," Ruth would say to God. "Henrietta said a lot of things in her day, but I didn't pay much attention to any of it. I expect she knew that."

FAITHFULLY DEPARTED

The sad truth is I was confused by, hung up on, a woman, and she was my wife of six years. She was lovely, and she tolerated me, barely. Just barely. She admitted it, said it as casually as if she were saying, "I like spinach," or "I drive a Ford," said she could not trust anyone, never had, never would. She cringed when I touched her; I knew it, had felt her shrink back, though she denied it, said my hurt feelings affected my perceptions. Besides, she asked, what did I think she was, a tube of toothpaste. I didn't have to squeeze so hard, did I? Eventually, I ran away. It was a spur-of-the-moment thing, my adult version of pulling the covers up over my head, and I did it because I needed a break like you do when nothing works and the one you love doesn't change and you start to forget how lucky you really are compared to the rest of the population, while self-pity sucks at you like quicksand.

"I like my hole-in-the-wall," I told my mother. "I've escaped into the still center of emotional turmoil."

"Rubbish," she said.

It was dusk on the one-year anniversary of Dad's death. Dad was Joe Baker and I was, too, only Junior. Joe Baker Junior, promoted to just plain old Joe by his death. The phone had been ringing when I entered my efficiency, and I almost didn't answer it in case it was Fred carrying the joke about how long it took me to solve a problem at work to a point far beyond funny. Instead, it was Mom.

"I never thought I'd raise such a selfish child," Mom said, causing me to briefly consider the child she referred to. He had not been selfish, I decided, but the man was. Me. Self-pity was selfish. I had moved to my hideout above the Thai food restaurant on Grand Boulevard, only blocks from my boyhood home, a scant mile from the Iron Street apartment Mom now lived in alone, to escape, to throw wide the French doors that opened onto the balcony with the loose wrought-iron rail, to listen to endless derivatives of *fuck,* day and night, to feel the building vibrate, and to say Glenda, Glenda, Glenda into the noise. Glenda was my wife.

I knew analyzing was as useless as it was boring. I knew it did not matter whether it was Glenda or I who had been improperly toilet trained, given too much or too little attention, been forced to eat our turnips and pickles. I didn't care if she was searching for a mother and I a father, or the other way around, or if what we both really needed was a devoted, flop-eared hound. Maybe she was an enchanted witch and I was a slimy toad. It didn't matter because I was lucky in keeping my job, lucky in having a few friends. Big deal if I was unlucky in love, in my wife. The assistant quality supervisor at Blackmun Box Company, *my* assistant and my friend Fred, said I was a rarity. He said only women put up with loneliness in their marriages. Only women married hoping to change the poor dumb slob.

Glenda had deep black eyes and skin like fine bone china. She was going to bring a pesto tart and a pâté to the party Mom was throwing on the anniversary of Dad's death. Mom was doing a turkey breast for small sandwiches, and all I was expected to bring was myself, the only son, the former Junior. It was all part of the grieving process, Mom said.

"I have my own process," I said, and she sighed. Some things she tried not to acknowledge, and a separate process was one. According to her, we—she and I—had never been depressed or angry or tired or bored or afraid or allergic to anything at all. Other people could be all those things, and I had been taught to be sympathetic but superior, knowing I would never be so afflicted. Mom did not accept my troubled marriage either, called my leaving foolishness. "It's just a break," I told Mom. "I just want to be alone and not so lonely."

"You're being melodramatic," Mom said then. "Childish."

That evening of her party for Dad's being dead for a year, I told her the city was big and loud, and I was submerged in it, covered over.

She said she'd see me at 7:30.

I had moved to my efficiency above the Thai food restaurant only two months before, had not meant to move until the day I came down here for lunch to celebrate Martha's retirement and saw the For Rent sign. "Excuse me," I said even before the drinks arrived and we toasted Martha, the best receptionist Blackmun Box ever had, we said, forty years of receiving, of being receptive, of receptivity. Even before Fred could give his speech, I went to the hostess's desk and was directed to a cook who made me sign a six-month lease and put a hundred down for security. "I'll move in tomorrow," I said.

"You're overreacting," Glenda said that evening when I told her. "But I won't make a scene."

"I don't expect a scene," I said. "You haven't even rehearsed."

So there I was on the anniversary of Dad's death, beginning my third month of escape. Glenda never had come by. "Don't pretend to care," I said when I called her the day after I moved. "You don't even miss me."

"Don't take it personally," she said. "I don't miss anyone."

"Hey, listen to this," I said to Mom on the evening of the anniversary of Dad's death. "I solved a problem today that could have cost us the Anheuser Busch account." I told her then about what Fred had been teasing me about. We had had a problem with separation caused by a glue with a high moisture content, and I'd been working for weeks on a process of joining layers that used more heat and so would dry out the glue faster without causing shrinkage or burning or warping. The Prez was getting annoyed at how long it was taking, and once I realized how simple it was, I was annoyed with myself, too. I didn't tell Mom the part about me being stupid, though, or about thinking as I pretended to enjoy Fred's jokes that I'd be better off selling onions and broccoli like Joe Senior. How could you screw that up?

I had thought Mom was listening, but when I finished, she asked if I thought one turkey breast would be enough.

"You really should broaden your interests," I said.

Mom had been down to my hideout just once, and that in broad daylight because the natives frightened her. She stood out on the sidewalk one Saturday in January and called, "Joe, Jo-jo. Help me up."

She was heavy, round, and pillow-like, and so had a hard time climbing the steep, narrow stairs to my hideout. The whole apartment was only seventeen by twenty. A sink, stove, and half-size refrigerator were squeezed in on one end, and a toilet and a shower stall were next to them, separated from the rest of the room by two louvered panels with a flowered curtain hanging between. The walls were covered by brown paper with a faint gold leaf design that seemed to keep the plaster in place. The floor was linoleum, also brownish. The room came with an olive drab hide-a-bed, a rust-colored overstuffed armchair, a white-painted wooden dinette table and two chairs, and two oak-veneer end tables with blue ceramic lamps screwed into their tops. There were tattered shades I never used on the French doors.

When I asked Mom what she thought, she said, "It should be padded. Anyone crazy enough to rent this needs padding. I suppose I should hide all your knives and forks.

"Seriously," she said. "I don't think your father would approve of your foolishness." My cheek muscle jumped once, just once.

"You've got it made," Dad, Joe Baker Senior, used to say. He said it to me, Joe Baker Junior, called Jo-jo as a child. Now that he was dead, I missed him as much as I had when he was alive.

When he was home, he and his buddies would sit on the stoop of the old two-story clapboard in the part of St. Louis so old it was called historic, a house I could have seen from my back window if I had had one. They'd drink beer, and Mom would join them, laughing at their jokes, telling a few of her own. He'd point at me. "Take my son," he'd say to his pals. "He's got it made. Not like me, not like I had it. He's got it made in the shade, got it knocked, got it laid out, got it licked, has beaten the world coming and going." Of course, he didn't say that all at once, or not usually, though he could carry on.

Once he drove me to a wrestling meet. I was in the ninth grade, and I wanted him to be one of those television dads—a pal, a teacher, a support. Any one of those would have done. It was one of the rare times we were alone in the car; I wondered where his buddies were. I was thankful we were alone, but nervous. "You know, Dad," I said. "I got the class award for my essay on the spread of communism."

He grunted. I tried again. "I think I'll be on the varsity wrestling team next year. Coach says I'll probably make it."

He nodded, keeping his eyes on the road.

"I don't know what I want to be when I grow up. I have to decide."

When he dropped me at the gymnasium, he turned and pointed at me. "You've got it made in the shade," he said above the loud idle of the engine. "Not like me. No sir. You've got the world by the short hairs." I could not tell if what he said made him happy or angry.

What he meant by the not-like-me part was a story Mom told often. He was the tail end of ten children, the ninth thirteen years old when he showed up as an afterthought, an accident. When he was three, his mother took rat poison, and four months later, his father was knifed in Tower Grove Park. He was raised by the older siblings, six months here, a year there, passed around like the queen of spades in a game of hearts, until he was sixteen and could quit school and go to work unloading trucks on produce row. He had enough to open his own store by the time he was twenty-four.

And he hated it. "What a life," he'd say to his buddies. "Watching the housefraus thump the melons day in and day out. Is this what I struggled for?" Listening to him, I learned to hate the store, too, and it was just as well because he never offered to let me in on it, didn't even try to get me to help out in summer. He may have thought he was doing me a favor, giving me one of the many breaks he knew I already had. Anyway, I think the tic in my right cheek surfaced around the ninth grade. It started out mild in the mornings, and grew more severe the longer I was awake. Many evenings, even before dusk, I felt chipmunks racing up and down inside my cheek, or my cheek cells re-enacting Custer's last stand.

After telling me it did not exist, that it was all in my head, that I should stop thinking about it, Mom finally broke down and took me to a few doctors. Over a two-year period, I was given muscle relaxers, antibiotics, tranquilizers, steroids, creams, and massages. Eventually, I agreed with Mom. The best thing to do was ignore it. It flared up so violently when I was engaged to Glenda that even people I hardly knew were giving me suggestions. Relax, work harder, find a hobby, drink red wine, don't drink at all, have your jaw aligned, drink more water, avoid spicy foods, keep away from nitrites, get an allergy-free pillow. Fred said I needed vitamin B-12, and the clerk in the license office said bee venom would work. Even Glenda deigned to say "poor thing" and offer a half-hearted suggestion of her own. Green tea was her idea. Of course, I tried it, gallons of it until she asked why I was drinking that stuff that smelled like a newly built outhouse.

Through it all, the tic persisted, almost gone now that I had escaped to my hiding place in the middle of the city.

For her party on the anniversary of Dad's death, Mom invited his old buddies, the ones he used to sit around on the stoop with, the ones he drank with at Trautman's and Pappy's, the guys who seemed to agree that his son had it made. She also invited Aunt Rose and her children, my three cousins, and their spouses and children. She invited Father Mullamphy and Beatrice from Holy Cross, Dad's parish for all his life, and Horace, the skinny guy who did her hair, and the couple who lived downstairs in the four-family Mom and Dad moved to when I went to college. Mom said the couple from downstairs wouldn't come, though, because the wife had a "nervous condition," the kind of thing I was not allowed. Some of Dad's old faithful customers were invited, as was his old Irish buddy, Donnelley. A professional Irishman, Dad called him. Two beers made him weepy. Aunt Rose was bringing cookies, and her daughter had promised a cheese ball.

"Will you be embarrassed that I'm not there?" I asked Mom that evening when she called to remind me to show up.

"I won't be embarrassed," she said. "Because you'll be here."

After Mom's call, I sat on my balcony and watched the pink sky above Pearl and Ray's Homecooking Restaurant across the street. At Mom's party, Glenda would treat me as a heartthrob, a lost love, a crush, a cherished life mate. I imagined she had been practicing her cry of delight and her tears of joy for days. I was thirty-seven, but around her I was fifteen. "Look, Glenda, no hands. See what I can do? Watch this. Pay attention." When we were alone, I felt like a piece of pink Double Bubble she wanted to scrape off her shoe, not serious but an annoyance. She only played to the house.

She worked out of our three-bedroom brick ranch in a safe, nice section of South County. She planned and coordinated conventions for large groups like building suppliers or Christian life activists. People she worked with, from the stand-up comics she hired to the CEOs that paid her, referred to her as warm, an example of real Midwestern friendliness. I fell for her when she planned the International Corrugated Packagers' Annual meeting six years ago.

I was thirty-one when I married, already supervising quality control audits for Blackmun, old enough, I thought then, not to make Mom's mistake of falling hard and never getting over it. "Isn't he wonderful?" Mom would ask me often, the two of us sitting down to watch the evening news while Dad kept the produce store open late, or the two of us hauling trash cans to the curb in the early morning, Joe Senior already open for the trucks bringing out-of-season greens from Mexico and California. "He always comes home to us," she'd say. "And he doesn't have to, you know. Lots of men don't."

"He doesn't like us," I said once, thinking myself wise after a high school class in psychology. "He can't be with just us. He always brings his friends."

We had been unloading the groceries and putting them away, but she stopped, a can of tomato sauce in each hand, and with her wrists on my shoulders, she turned me to face her. "Don't go looking for trouble," she said.

Later, I learned about the other women.

"Here's a question for you," I said to Glenda when we were first dating, making fun of my younger self to entertain her. "If an underage boy spots his father in a cocktail lounge, kissing a strange woman, does he say anything?"

"Don't get pathetic on me," she said. I would have dragged out all my family skeletons for her entertainment, but she said, "Nothing bores me more than men who cheat. I mean, who cares?"

She was divorced, and her first husband, an heir to a building fortune, was often romantically linked in the *St. Louis Post-Dispatch* gossip column with prominent lawyers, fragile-looking women holding endowed chairs in bioethics, or the symphony's first violinist. I knew he had cheated on Glenda, so I pitied her, promised her a life of love and trust. "I'll never be unfaithful to you," I said.

"Oh boy," she said, and rolled her eyes.

＊

As I said, I liked my new neighborhood, not exactly deteriorating, because that was past, deteriorated already and according to a few optimists, on the way back up. I slept on the hide-a-bed and kept the French doors open any night it was above freezing. I liked the sounds of fights and screams and laughs and sirens, of taunts and jokes and the clanking of trucks and the squealing of tires. A maelstrom of emotions grew and swirled outside. Humans at their truest.

"Get out of there," Fred said. "One minute you'll be sitting on your balcony, and the next, Kapow, you'll be picked off."

But I was a city kid, and the city was a living thing to me, an entity the way mountainsides and oceans were to others. Tree frogs and crickets and owls made as much noise as my mostly down-and-out neighbors who beat on each other then begged forgiveness, as the yuppies or muppies or whatever they were called who came in from their gated communities to eat unpronounceable soup downstairs at the Moeng Tai, as the leftover hippies and resurrected Beats who gave voice to their angst at the coffee houses named *The Grinder* and *Espresso Express*. I had no radio, no television, no boom box. The street was enough.

The main smell in my efficiency was that of the lemon grass, garlic, and shallots that permeated the wood and bricks and asbestos and lead paint that sheltered me. I thought if I went to Mom's party for the anniversary of Dad's death, I would take the prawn salad made with bird's eye chilies and a few orders of the fish balls called *Tad Mun Pla*. The evening before, I'd gone down for a pound of seven spice beef, and I still had most of it left, so I could take that as well.

Even after the pink disappeared above Pearl and Ray's Home-cooking Restaurant across Grand, the night air was warm for February, so I stayed on my balcony. The day we buried Dad, three days after he died last year, was warm, too. A hint of spring. I listened to the daytime hum turn into a nighttime hum, a hum with an edge, a higher pitched hum. I closed my eyes and felt a rock hit my chest. I heard a woman's voice. "Wake up."

I looked at the rock on my balcony, then down at the sidewalk.

"Wake up," the woman said again. She was standing under a streetlight, looking up and talking to me.

"I am awake," I said, leaning carefully over the railing I knew was loose. She was short and thin, skeletal almost, her face made sharper by the tight blondish ponytail that seemed to pull it back. She held a white-haired woman by the hand. Both women wore loose, dark dresses that seemed to hang to their ankles, and the younger one carried a tattered straw hat in her other hand. "What's up?" I asked. "What do you want?"

"Money," the younger one said. "We're hungry. Can't you tell it's dinnertime?"

"Wait," I said. I was used to being asked, had given sandwiches to the ones who wore signs saying they would work for food, dollars to those who wanted Big Macs, fives and tens to those with the highly improbable stories of families stranded on the highways, wife and children waiting in the broken-down car. Once a guy ran out of Dad's old haunt, Pappy's, as I walked by, yelling, "Hey, Sport." I stopped and he told me he had lost his bus money and needed to get home. I gave, of course, and had since seen him pull the same ploy every Friday night. I figured he took in fifteen or twenty a Friday, and that was only if he got just a dollar a piece. Still, it was rough work, hard and dangerous, and I liked to think he would rather have had a job at the box company.

So when the two women called up, I knew I'd help. Instead of digging my meager stash from my billfold, though, I decided to give them the beef. I made four thick sandwiches, wrapped them in foil, put them and two dollar bills for sodas in a plastic grocery bag, and carefully dropped it over the railing.

"Thanks, Bub," the younger woman said. "But we wanted money. That way we can chose our own food."

You know what they say beggars can't be, I wanted to remind her, but instead I explained she couldn't find a place anywhere near with beef that good. People drove in from all over the county to wait in line for the specially spiced beef.

"We're vegetarians," she said. "Beef is bad for our lipid count."

"Well," I said. "I don't have much money, but I can give you a few more dollars." I reached back for my billfold, but she stopped me.

"We're homeless," she said. "Any idiot could tell that. Can we come up and use your bathroom, wash our faces? It would mean so much."

"Wait there," I said. I went down the steep narrow steps to the street door, unlocked it, and let them in. I helped the older woman by holding her arm, pulling gently when I had to. I decided I would take them across the street to Pearl and Ray's Homecooking Restaurant, after they washed up. They would be part of my grieving process.

"Are you the lifeguard?" the younger one asked as we helped the older one up the stairs.

"What?"

"You sit out there like the lifeguard. We've seen you before. Will you dive down if you see trouble?"

As soon as they were in my room, even before I could point to the curtain hiding the toilet and shower, the younger one said "Stop." I had turned my back on her to close the upstairs door, and when I turned around, I saw the gun. It was a small one, thick but short. A .32. She must have had it under the broken-brimmed straw hat.

No one had ever pointed a gun at me, and my knees turned to slush. My cheek muscles imitated Mexican jumping beans. "I don't have much money here," I said, and my voice was a whisper. I could not tell if she heard.

"Are you trying to trap us?" she asked.

I shook my head. "Can I sit?"

"Because it won't work. I haven't slept in years. I stay awake to protect her." She nodded at the older one. "She's all I got in the world. And I'm the only one she can trust."

I sat on the couch. I knew I should have been making a plan, should have had an adrenaline rush or some such that would keep me alive, but I felt only light, all finished. Would I die on the anniversary of Dad's death, Senior and Junior going exactly one year apart? Only one of them had had it made. Glenda would be a beautiful widow, her thin shoulders shaking slightly as she sobbed in her designer black crepe de chine.

The younger one pushed the older one down into the over-stuffed chair, never taking her eyes off me.

"Is that loaded?" I asked.

"Are you calling me stupid?"

"No," I said.

"Why did you lure us up here?" she asked.

"It was your idea."

"Ha! That beef was poison, right?"

"No."

She sat on the arm of the chair. "I found this gun. Some dirtbag threw it in a trash can. What day is this?"

"It's the anniversary of Dad's death," I said.

"Oh, boo hoo," she said. "Don't try for sympathy. What day is this?"

"Thursday."

"Where's your money? Why haven't you given it to me yet?"

"I have only about fifteen in my billfold. That's it." I reached back, and she stood, moved closer, her gun inches from my chest. "Take it," I said as I got my billfold free. She did.

"What's wrong? Are you a bum?"

I shook my head.

"I guess I'll have to kill you," she said.

"Why?"

She sounded impatient. "I'm robbing you, for one thing. *And* you tricked us up here. *And* you tried to poison us. *And* if you had a gun, you'd shoot us."

"No," I said, my will returning. Could I wrest the gun from her before she could fire?

"Who killed your dad?"

"No one," I said. "God."

"We don't believe in God," she said. "If we did, we'd be really pissed at him."

"I don't blame you," I said. Was it true that if they kept talking, they wouldn't shoot? "I understand," I said, knowing it sounded fake.

"Do you think I'm pretty?"

"Absolutely."

"We don't want to use your bathroom," she said.

"You could if you wanted to."

"We're natural. We go on the street, wherever."

"Might as well," I said.

"But you think I'm pretty. And I'm not even wearing makeup. If I had a better dress on, you'd probably make a pass at me."

"I wouldn't be surprised," I said.

"You're no fool," she said.

"Neither are you," I said. "That's why you won't shoot."

"But we believe in abortion," she said. "All kinds. Even retroactive. Like you. We could abort you now. Pow!" She lifted her arm after her pretend shot as if from the recoil. I guessed her experience of shooting came from television. Like mine. It gave me some hope.

"My name's Joe," I said. "So was my dad's."

"Mine, too," she said, sitting again on the arm of the chair, blocking my view of the old woman.

"My mother's observing the anniversary of his death tonight." I hoped talk was better than silence.

"Mine, too," she said.

"Finger food, not sit down," I said. "Her apartment's too small."

"Right," she said.

"My wife claims to love me, but is just as happy without me around."

"Understandable," she said.

"Her name's Glenda," I said.

"Does that hurt?" she asked.

"What?"

"Your face is dancing."

"It's an odd sensation," I said.

"What isn't?" she asked, and sighed. Then she was quiet for so long, I thought she may actually have been waiting for an answer.

I finally spoke. "You're not really going to shoot me, are you?"

"Why not?"

"Is that your mother with you?"

"None of your business."

"Do you think she'd like to see someone die?"

"She saw Brother die," she said.

"And?"

"She cried."

"Like now?" I asked, and when she looked behind her, I lunged across the room, hit her in the side, and knocked her to the floor. She dropped the gun, and I grabbed it. She was even lighter than she looked, but the gun was heavy. And warm. I pointed it at her. She sat on the floor, shaking her hand around in front of her face. The older one still sat in the chair, looking at her lap. My room smelled of urine.

"You hurt me," the one on the floor said.

"I'll have to call the police," I said, standing above her, the gun trained on her chest.

She stood. "You could have just given us some money," she said. "All this trouble because we're vegetarians."

"Stay where you are," I said.

"Come on," she said to the older one, who stood, the chair cushion now a darker shade of rust.

"You can't go," I said. "I'm calling the police."

"Bye," she said, and opened my top door.

"I'll shoot," I said as she helped the older one down the stairs.

"No you won't," she said.

I picked up my billfold from the floor, called the police, and as I awaited their arrival, I sat on the balcony and watched the two move down Grand, all the way to Hartford, then turn right. The police were more interested in the gun than in picking up the two women. "We know where to find them," the older of the pair said to me. And yes, the gun was loaded. The older officer asked if I was related to the Joe Baker who used to run the produce store. I said yes. He said it was a shame we closed it after Dad died. He said he heard it was going to be a 7–11. I told him he had heard right.

It was nearly 8:30 by the time they left. After coming close to death, I expected to be filled with a renewed sense of life, to be able to feel my irises open and close, feel the cilia covering my lungs sway in the breeze of each inhale, hear the hair in my ears grow. But all I heard and felt was my heart. It bumped, thumped, and jerked, threw itself against my rib cage violently, as if trying to make a break for it. I had a pulse in my stomach and my feet and my neck all at once.

✳

By the time I got there, Mom's apartment was packed with people who wanted to give Dad one last send-off, people for whom the wake had been only a prelude, and I had a hard time squeezing into the living room. I bumped right into Mom in the process, making her spill her beer all down her new blue suit. She hugged me. "I knew you'd make it." Her face was flushed, and she sounded breathless.

"I was almost killed tonight," I said.

"Shhh," she said. "Here comes Aunt Rose." Aunt Rose wanted me to try the fudge brownies and tell her if they were sweet enough, and Horace the hairdresser appeared and asked if

Blackmun still had the Anheuser Busch contract. We did, I told him. He said it must be an important one, and I agreed it was. He nodded and winked at me as if he had just taught me something, let me in on a corporate secret. My pulse was in my tongue by then, so I just nodded back. I saw Glenda across the room, laughing at something the man from downstairs with the "nervous" wife had said. She had had her hair cut, and her short black curls shone in the light of Mom's heirloom silver candelabra. My cheek muscles jumped in time with my pulse.

When she finally spotted me I was at the dining-room table, and she let loose a throaty cry and gave me a movie-star hug. "I just knew you wouldn't stay away," she said to the crowd. My cheek did the mambo.

"I thought you two were separated," Beatrice, the housekeeper from Holy Cross, said.

"Poor Joe has been having some problems," Glenda said to Beatrice and everyone else. "Some of them have to do with his grieving process. But we're working through them together."

"That's the way," Old Man Donnelley said. "For better or worse." He nudged me and whispered. "You've got it made, Son."

"I would have been here sooner," I said, "but I was held up at gunpoint." No one seemed to have heard.

"I hope we don't run out of pâté," Glenda said to Beatrice.

"Let's have a toast," the man from downstairs shouted, and Mom, still in the living room, called for silence. Then Old Man Donnelley gave a long-winded one about when the devil knows you're dead and where the wind and sun are in relation to you. I thought he said it all at least twice.

Then we bowed our heads as Father Mullamphy led us in a prayer for Dad's soul and the souls of all the faithful departed.

Old Man Donnelley's daughter stood beside me and put her arm under my blazer and around my waist. She was old enough to have been my babysitter once or twice, and she looked even older close up. Delicate, purple puffs lay under each eye, but she fit nicely against my side as she leaned into me, and her hair smelled like mushrooms.

"I was almost killed tonight," I said.

"You must feel lucky to be alive," she said, tightening her hug, pulling me even closer. My skin burned through my shirt at her touch.

"I am lucky," I said.

"Something like that must make you want to get all you can out of life."

"It does," I whispered into her petal-shaped ear.

"It must make you want to live it up," she whispered back.

"Yes," I said. "I want to."

CREDITS

The following stories, in slightly different form, have appeared elsewhere: "Divine Light," *River Styx;* "King Herod Died of Cancer," *Ascent;* "The Poet's Daughter," *Delmar 5;* and "Henrietta," *American Fiction No. 2.*

ABOUT THE AUTHOR

Mary Troy, a St. Louis native, teaches creative writing at the University of Missouri–St. Louis.